AF230705

MEDLEY

Songs of life, a couple out of tune

Bella Karoli

ISBN: 978-1-64970-027-8   (Paperback Edition)
ISBN: 978-1-64970-028-5   (Hardcover Edition)
ISBN: 978-1-64970-026-1   (E-book Edition)

Some characters and events in this book are fictitious. Any similarity to real persons, living or dead, is coincidental and not intended by the author.

Book Ordering Information

Phone Number: 347-901-4929 or 347-901-4920
Email: info@globalsummithouse.com
Global Summit House
www.globalsummithouse.com

Printed in the United States of America

Table of Contents

Dedication

This book is dedicated to God, Who gave me the talent, and to my partner and best friend Tom Burch, who gave me the support and encouragement for what it took to finish this project.

A sincere "Thank you!" to both of them!

Introduction

I have been writing since third grade. Mostly I do short stories, but there are also poetry, music and song lyrics, a budding novel in the works, and right now, four short stories that I am working on simultaneously. Although there is another book that was printed seven years ago and can be found on my web site through Global Summit House, nothing really came of it.

This is a collection of short stories that were written at various times over the last umpteen years. Interruptions caused the writing breaks, but I see myself more as a musician than a writer. However, if an appealing idea pops in, I will sit down immediately and start writing. I usually don't know where the stories are going, and with a couple in this collection, there were surprises along the way. The story ideas are not usually thought out completely beforehand. There are the ideas of what needs to be said at the beginning and perhaps in the middle somewhere, and sometimes the ending, but usually the story writes itself. I'm just the transcriber.

This collection is quite varied. From lighthearted to very serious, like a fairy tale to snippets of how cruel the world can be. They reflect events and thoughts of our lives, pleasant and unpleasant surprises. Some were written while being a member of the River Writers in Arizona.

Even if He isn't mentioned directly, God is in them. If you don't believe in God or believe in a different one, what is here is found in mankind generally. I just happen to have this particular view.

The stories are meant to be enjoyed. You might even learn something from them. They are not really meant to teach anything, but one can always learn a thing or two while reading whatever suits their fancy. My publisher wants more, so I shall oblige. But for now, just enjoy!

The Drop

Maude Wasserman first noticed the package at the side of the road only after she'd driven by one like it for a month. It caught her attention because there was something different about it, something she couldn't place. It seemed to her she'd seen a package often before, but it hadn't registered. This one, for some reason, stood out. She wondered if she'd see a package again tomorrow, or the day after that. She decided to pay attention to this particular stretch of the highway the next day.

Maude drove a small SUV for a mail and package company. Her late afternoon route took her from the rapidly growing city of Silver Point along the desert highway to the small town of Quin's Gap, a thirty-five-mile drive of sand, cacti, rock formations, cattle fencing, and scrub, with foothills and mountains set back a ways back from the road. Quin's Gap had three gas stations, a general store, a motel, a tiny casino with great food, a few nondescript houses, and a nondescript museum of sorts that portrayed the mining history of the area. For a dollar, you could ride a quarter of a mile in a mining car into the side of the hill – it was too small for a mountain – where you could pan for "gold" (pyrite) or dig a pit for silver nuggets, thoughtfully left there by the real miners in the mountains four miles east. A small gift shop selling jewelry made by local Indians and Gap residents completed the town, a break in the trip from Silver Point to River Valley fifty miles farther south.

Maude made a point of looking for the package at about the same place she'd seen it the day before, approximately ten miles north of the Gap, as the little town was called for short. There was nothing, but after dropping off her mail, picking up the outgoing, and having a quick bite at the casino café, she returned with curiosity piqued and a desire to know what the package contained. However, the area still was devoid of string-tied objects, so she had to satisfy her curiosity another day.

The third day, on her way to the Gap, she saw a bright blue lump resting against one of the fence posts. She slowed to a speed that was as safe as traffic allowed and tried to see as much of it as she could. It seemed to be about the size of a small duffle bag and interestingly bumpy. *Somehow,* she thought, *it doesn't seem to be very heavy. I'm going to keep my eye on this. I know I'm too nosy, but I have to know what's going on. No one else seems to notice. Maude, none of your business. Watch out! That jerk just cut in front of me!* "Jackass!" she exclaimed aloud, embarrassed to know that if she hadn't been gawking at the blue object, she wouldn't have almost collided with the other car. So she didn't know if the exclamation had been for the other driver or her. Or both.

Somewhat shaken, Maude concentrated on traffic until her arrival at the general store, the mail's pickup point. Old Man Moe was behind the counter as usual, mail in the tub at the corner of the counter. Moe, his trademark shock of white hair and questionably clean apron flapping as he spoke, was having an intense discussion with a traveler. Maude picked up her tub and replaced it with the one delivered. She wanted to ask Moe's wife, Daisie, about something but didn't see her anywhere. As she was leaving, Moe called to her.

"Hey, Maudie girl!" His rich baritone voice reverberated throughout the store. "C'mere! This here fella's got a question fer ya!"

"Hey, Moe, how goes it?" Maude grinned as she turned back to the men. The traveler, not more than twenty, wore new hiking gear and a frustrated face. "How can I help you?" she asked him.

"I thought you people would know everything about this area, but this old geezer doesn't seem to understand that I'm looking for the Playa mine, which is supposed to be at the mountain close by. My map clearly shows it! I want to hike there and up the mountain, right here!" He pointed to a spot on his brand new map.

"May I?" Maude asked, putting down the tub and indicating the map. The man didn't let go but turned it so she could see. "Here! See for yourself! PLAYA MINE, in big, bold letters. One of the best silver mines in the state, its output hundreds of thousands of dollars per year! I've got to see an operation like that! Maybe you can set this old guy straight!"

Maude glanced at Moe, who was turning red, and winked. She'd been studying the map as the young man spoke, and knew what he was looking for. He wouldn't find it, however.

"Sir," she said seriously, "you are correct that the Playa Mine has put out a goodly amount of silver worth what you say. Did it for years. I assume you got this map at Smith's Trek and Deck in River Valley?"

"Of course! It's the best in the area! All experienced hikers go there!"

"Hm. Well, that lets you out, then. I see by your outfit that you ain't a cowboy, and you ain't much of a hiker either, or you would have recognized that this map is a newly printed COPY of the original from 1937. Everything that's on it is still there except the mine. It petered out over forty years ago and now lets tourists such as yourself dig for silver from an old pit fed small, cheap nuggets from what's left of the original mine. So if you want to see the operations of the Playa Mine, you'll have to watch the video at the gift shop next to its replica at the hill a quarter-mile from here. You pays your dollar at the museum on Second Street and rides in an old mine car to the site." Maude picked up the tub. "Happy digging, and don't get them fancy new duds dirty!" She nodded at Moe, who was having little success at hiding a huge grin. "Tell Daisie I said hi, and I may have some interesting scuttlebutt for her tomorrow!" She left the young man staring after her, mouth open, and burst into a laugh as soon as the door closed behind her.

Traffic was light as Maude pulled away, still chuckling at the "dude's" ignorance. Hiker, indeed. Thinking about him and his "fancy duds" during the drive back almost made her miss what she was looking for. Almost. If a dark blue car that contrasted with the surroundings hadn't been parked on the shoulder, she would have sailed right past it. Unfortunately, traffic didn't let her stop to check it out. Now her curiosity really spiked. That was a brand new vehicle. It looked expensive. Why was it parked at the package site? What was in that package? A glance in the rearview mirror told her nothing, but the car was now flashing a turn signal, indicating that it was about to leave. She hadn't seen anyone, and this annoyed her. *Why am I annoyed? It's none of my business what goes on out here.*

Trying not to let it be her business, Maude concentrated on the out-of-state plate and general configuration of the '55 Lincoln ahead of her.

The next couple of weeks were spent trying to figure it out. Several more packages of varying colors appeared at the post, and sometimes Maude saw the dark blue vehicle parked there. She took the license number but wasn't really sure what to do with it. Daisie met with her a few times, and their tongues wagged nonstop. They tried to make sense of it. Once, Maude saw the blue car pull away from the site and a smaller light green car pull up. She slowed enough to be able to catch a glimpse of a woman getting out and moving toward this time pale yellow package, but could not stop to see anything else. Now Maude was really into it. She was sure that something illegal was going on, most likely a drug deal; otherwise, why go through the trouble of hiding something in the open? She didn't know what the colors of the packages meant, or even if they meant anything, and decided to do some sleuthing on her own. Or with Daisie, if her friend was willing to hide out in the desert shrubbery some dark night. Maude would see with her own eyes what was "going down," as her grandchildren would say; if only she could figure out how to get the police to be there as well and catch the dealers red-handed.

"That's a plan, but don't you have to have actual proof first?" Daisie asked when Maude requested her presence and told her what she thought. They sat with coffee in Daisie's kitchen.

"We can get it when the package is dropped off," Maude replied. "It's getting dark sooner now, and in a couple of weeks, it will be dark at the time of the drop-off. We can hide behind some of the thick bushes, and if we wear black, we won't be noticed. We will see who drops off the package, who picks it up, and I can get the license number of the second car from where I plan to hide. We'll be inside the wire fenced area, so no one should see us."

"Where are you going to park the car?"

"There's a back road that's been closed to traffic for years stretching from Quin's Gap through the fenced-off area; we can take that and leave the car there; it's about a half-mile walk to the road. If we are lucky, the moon won't be out that night, and –"

"Hold it!" Daisie interrupted. "You are expecting me to dress like a burglar in all black, take an old beat-up road that nobody's been on in a decade and then walk half a mile in the dark through the desert? Are you out of your cotton-pickin' mind, old girl!? That sounds totally crazy to me!" She looked askance at Maude. "You are obsessed, you know! Why are you poking your nose into this weird affair? You could get hurt or killed out there! Ever think of that?"

"Not at all," Maude replied, in a voice that indicated she wasn't about to start thinking of it now. "Look, someone put something there, and someone else picked it up. Who besides a drug dealer or someone passing contraband stuff would do such a thing? I mean, who besides someone who has something to hide does stuff like that?"

"You've been watching too many cops and robbers shows," Daisie interrupted.

Maude continued as if Daisie had said nothing. "Granted, the car the guy drives is uber-noticeable, but only at certain times of the day. At night, it's hard to see. I drove right past it yesterday and didn't realize it until five miles later. And you know we're not that far from the border. That's a pretty wild area out there, and even though there's a lot of traffic on the highway, it's only at certain hours, and drivers stop along that road for all kinds of reasons. Nobody thinks anything of it to see a car on the shoulder. For all they know, the driver is waiting for a cop or something. There are a few patrols at night, you know."

"Yes, and what if one of them decides to investigate US?" Daisie shot back.

"We'll tell the truth – that something fishy is going on, and we wanted to put a stop to it."

"Make that *you*."

"Oh, come on, Daisie, there's nothing to worry about. We'll be safe. We'll have flashlights and carry pepper spray or mace for protection in case one of the dealers should catch us."

"And if they find out we're two old ladies making like Batman and Robin, do you really think we're going to be safe? We'd be lucky not to have them shoot us on the spot! And how do we RUN half a mile back to the car?"

They argued back and forth, and in the end, Daisie gave in. She checked the Farmer's Almanac to see when the next moonless night would be, and they settled on six o'clock the following Thursday. Maude flashed her friend a smile and gave her an enthusiastic thumbs up. Daisie stuck out her tongue and reminded Maude that she was illegal because she hadn't yet returned to Silver Point with the day's mail.

"I'll sort it when I get back; it doesn't go out until tomorrow morning, anyway, when the big truck stops to pick everything up."

"Maude, you have an answer for everything except why you let Mary Lou Washburn steal Dale Fisher when you know darn well he wanted to marry you!"

"But I got a better deal with Herb Wasserman. Yeah, he was a little old for me, but you'd never know it where it mattered!"

The two women parted with a laugh and a hug.

Maude decided that Daisie had made some good points and convinced herself that a dry run alone might be in order. So Sunday morning, early, she drove her car to Quin's Gap, found the old neglected road, blew out a tire, lost a hubcap, and threw the front end out of alignment on her way to and from the place where she intended to park it. As it limped back to the Gap to get the tire changed, she also changed her mind about other things. If this were going to be done, it would be done right.

Thursday night, a rented all-wheel-drive Jeep pulled up in front of Daisie's house. Black. With dark tinted windows. With a mechanic's tool chest behind the driver's seat. And Herb Wasserman, a master mechanic, also in black, seated in that very seat.

"I thought this was going to be just the two of us!" Daisie exclaimed. "Evenin', Herb!"

"Daisie." Herb grinned and tipped an invisible hat.

"It is just us," Maude said. "Herb will stay in the car. If we get in trouble, I'll signal with the flashlight, and he'll drive over and rescue us."

Daisie rolled her eyes and made a "you're hopeless" face, which Maude did not see.

Forty-five minutes later, the two women were seated on the ground behind a creosote bush. The lights from the cars on the highway allowed them to see pretty well, so it was easy to spot the dark blue vehicle when it pulled up. They tensed. A well-dressed man got out of the car, leaving the motor running, and walked around the front carrying something under his arm. He looked around and placed the package against the post, letting out a strange melodic whistle. Then he got back into the car and drove off.

The women were excited.

"Daisie! Did you hear that whistle?! It sounded like a gang signal!" Maude's voice sounded breathy with the stage whisper.

"I did!" Daisie whispered back. "I wonder how many will show up?"

"Probably just one," Maude whispered back. She was quieter now. "We can't talk. Sound travels well at night because it's quieter out here." She looked around but could not see the Jeep. It was in the shadow of rocks the distance of five city blocks back. The moonless night certainly was the appropriate time to be here.

"How long do you think we'll have to wait?" Daisie whispered as quietly as she could.

"Don't know. Let's be quiet now."

They settled back down. Traffic gradually thinned out until there was only the occasional car. The temperature dropped to shivering. Then the wind started. No one had come for the package.

Maude became frustrated. She hated giving up, but it appeared that was the only thing to do for the night. Then a thought hit her.

"I'm going to get that package," she whispered to Daisie.

"Are you sure?" Maude heard the alarm in her friend's voice. "What if –"

"Nobody came, and nobody's coming. There are no cars. I'm going to do it!"

Carefully, she stretched first, stiff from sitting so long. A bone cracked. She slipped out from behind the creosote bush, and half waddled, half crawled to the post. She grabbed the package and was surprised at its weight. Startled, she paused for a moment.

Maude was about to return when a slight noise about ten feet behind froze her in place.

The hair on the back of her head stood on end. Fear permeated her body. *Thinking* about being brave and firing mace certainly was different than actually *being* brave… while remembering the mace container lying on the front seat of the Jeep, right where she'd put it after taking it out of her pants pocket because she'd sat on it.

The noise came closer. It was now about eight feet away. Now six. Maude shivered violently and tried to keep her teeth from falling from her mouth, they were chattering so hard. Then her heart stopped beating as a soft, low growl emanated from the darkness.

Oh, my God. The gang member had a dog. She pictured a ferocious pit bull with spiked teeth and a heavy chain on a similarly spiked collar being held back by a six-foot-six gorilla, not recognizable because of the bandanna across his face underneath the backward cap he wore, showing just enough eye to be able to see.

There was another growl. Or was it the gorilla mumbling, "Give me that before I drill you." Or maybe "kill you"?

Maude very slowly put the package on the ground to her right and carefully, inch by agonizing inch, moved away from it about three feet to her left. There was a sudden rush as the animal grabbed the package and sped back in the direction from which it came.

Maude waited until her heartbeat resumed to something resembling normal, then scrambled back on all fours to Daisie.

"What was it!?" she gasped. "Did you see it? Did you see the gorilla with the huge pit bull? Did he have a gun? Which way did he go because I want to go in the exact opposite!?"

Daisie hugged her friend. "Calm down, Maude, there was no gorilla, nor did I see a pit bull. Only a thin coyote running for his life with the package in his mouth."

"He stole it!" Maude wailed. "All this waiting and a coyote stole the package!" She slammed her fist into the sand. "I was so scared, Daisie! All I could think about was I was going to die at the hands of a gorilla and a pit bull! And here a coyote steals the package! I hope he gets so stoned he turns into a rock!" Maude burst into tears on Daisie's shoulder.

She let her friend cry out the fear and frustration. Then very calmly, she said, "Let's go back now. We've had enough for one night. For the rest of my life, anyway."

Slowly, they helped each other up. Daisie flashed the light toward what she hoped was the direction of the truck. Fog lights gradually enlarged and came closer. Finally, Herb helped his wife into the back seat while he got into the driver's seat. He tossed the mace onto the dashboard so Daisie could sit and readjusted himself.

"Let's go home, ladies." The Jeep slipped into gear and bounced into the darkness, not seeing where it was going until they were back on the beat-up road. Headlights flashed on, lighting the way to hot coffee and warm blankets.

Maude stayed in bed all day Friday and half the day on Saturday. By Sunday, she'd recovered enough to begin rethinking her strategy.

All that week, she ignored the post. If the package were there, she didn't notice. Her brain was too busy planning another approach.

The following Friday, she parked about thirty yards from the post and waited, headlights out, overhead lights on, pretending to read a map. Shortly after dark, the blue car moved slowly past her, stopping at its usual place. Again, a man got out, put the package against the post, and whistled. Then he got back into the car and drove away.

Maude waited twenty minutes. Her headlights went on just in time to catch a dog-like figure slip its head under the bottom wire of the fence, grab the package, and run. She got out of the car, hoping to get a glimpse of where the animal went, but it had already disappeared. Disappointed,

Maude decided that the next night she would get the elusive package before anyone or anything else showed up.

She almost did. Parked in the same place, again pretending to read a map, she saw the blue car slip past her silently and stop about fifty feet in front of her. The man got out, dropped off the package, and drove away. She was about to start her car when a red Mustang pulled in front of her, a passenger got out, retrieved the package, and got back in. The car roared away before she could even turn the key.

Maude got mad. She started her car and leaped into traffic, spraying gravel and sand behind her as she entered the highway. Gradually, she got close enough to the Mustang to get its license plate number. She put the pedal to the metal and sped past it, disappearing around a curve while the two people in the car wondered what that was all about.

Two miles down the road, they placidly drove past a frustrated female driver gesturing to and hollering at a state trooper, who was writing something on a pad. He handed it to her, touched his cap, and strolled back to his vehicle, shaking his head.

The next day, Maude went to the state police office in Silver Point and explained to a disinterested officer what she had seen and done over the last few weeks, leaving out the part about receiving a speeding ticket the night before. The officer took the piece of paper with the two license numbers on it and said he'd run a check on them. Politely thanking her for her report, he ushered Maude out and said he'd take care of it.

Somehow, Maude didn't quite believe it. Whether it was the tone of voice, the apparent lack of interest or the lack of jumping right onto something she believed was of the utmost importance, Maude was not convinced the officer would actually do something. Well, she'd take care of that problem herself. She had enough frustration over the drops and decided direct action was the best solution.

Despite Daisie's earlier concerns, Maude never stopped to think about what could happen if this indeed were a drug deal and the driver of the blue car decided to take care of *his* problem in an unofficially official way. She never thought about any consequences whatsoever. She would catch the driver in the act and make a citizen's arrest. When the second car came to pick up the package, she would arrest him, too. *How* to accomplish this feat and *with what* never crossed her mind.

As it turned out, she needn't have worried – not that Maude ever wasted any energy on that. A few nights later, everything fell neatly into place. Maude was "map reading" when the blue car floated past hers and parked in its usual place. The man got out, looked around, placed the package on the ground next to the post, and whistled. Only this time, he stayed put, looking into the desert, which tonight was lit by a bright moon. Excited, Maude turned off the overhead light and slowly drove to within a few feet of the blue car. The man took no notice. He stared into the desert emptiness, appearing to be looking for something. He did not seem to be aware that Maude had gotten out of her car and was approaching from behind until, in her best official Post Office voice, she loudly stated, "You're under arrest! Anything you say can and will be used against you in a court of law! Place your hands on the post and do not move!"

The man did as she said, still not appearing to be concerned. Indeed, his concern continued to be the desert. He whistled again. There was silence, except for the vehicles that whizzed past.

Maude was elated. This was going completely according to her idea! Only she had no idea what to do next. Her knowledge of arrests was based on television police shows, which generally followed a form: according to them, a backup would suddenly appear. Maude looked around. At the moment, theirs were the only two cars in sight.

She looked at the man. He was standing there, hands on the post as commanded, but not paying any attention to her. Not only that, but up close, his presence was a lot more commanding than she was prepared for. He was several inches taller than her five-foot-six, with broad shoulders and, as Maude became aware, the sports jacket he wore appeared to be extra-large, which meant that not only was there a heavy woolen sweater under it because of the cold, the arms in the sleeves contained muscles. Large ones, most likely. While not a weakling, Maude realized her slender arms were no match for his big ones. In fact, the more she became aware of the man's physical presence, the more her idea of a citizen's arrest seemed to be incomplete.

Not only that, but a second car also pulled up behind Maude's (effectively blocking her in, as she noted with some trepidation), and the woman she'd seen before emerged. The woman was also tall, and even in the moonlight, Maude could see that the coat she wore was expensive. She decided that even though they may be illegal, dealers didn't waste money on cheap clothes. The woman came to them and asked the man, "What's going on here?"

"I believe we're under arrest," he replied calmly. "Apparently, our drop-off scheme attracted this upstanding citizen's attention, and she has ordered me to place my hands on the post and not move, which, as you see, I am doing." He had not changed position but continued to look into the desert.

Maude suddenly remembered her purpose and commanded the woman to do the same. They looked at each other, and then the woman silently complied, striding to the post and placing her hands over those of the man. He acknowledged the gesture with a nod but did not look at her.

"Now what?" she asked Maude.

"Now we wait for the state troopers," Maude stated with authority. "They should be here shortly."

Actually, Maude had not thought of telling anyone about her plan and now had no idea what to do.

However, just like on television, backup suddenly appeared in the form of two state trooper cars. Her righteousness resettled itself firmly, and courage took over. As the troopers approached, Maude said with authority, "Gentlemen, arrest these perps! I caught them red-handed and flatfooted! There on the ground is your evidence."

A trooper stood next to Maude, and his eyes went to where she pointed. Sure enough, under the plain brown paper this time, sat the lumpy "evidence."

"I'll have to admit, you're brave," another cop said. A total of four now clustered around her. "How long have you been keeping these folks under surveillance?"

Maude thought for a moment. "Well, maybe fifteen, twenty minutes tonight. From the first time I saw a package here, about two months. I drive this highway daily, except weekends, and out of sixty days, I'd say there was something here about fifty, with different colored papers each time, but I don't know whether or not that means anything. The colors could be a code as to how much drugs or drug money is wrapped in there. I've seen the woman" – Maude gestured toward the expensive coat – "pick-up the packages on several occasions. I've also seen them stolen by a coyote that slips under the wire and makes off with them. That's happened quite a few times now."

The woman looked at Maude, astonished. "A coyote!?" she exclaimed.

"Good!" the man responded. He also turned to Maude. "I'm glad you confirmed that! I was hoping for that response!"

"HUH?" Maude's eyes flew open. "You're giving drugs to a coyote?? Isn't that animal cruelty?" She turned to the troopers. "There! You see? More evidence that these are nasty folks! Giving drugs to animals!"

Everyone laughed.

"Do you know who this is?" the first trooper chuckled.

Maude drew herself up to her full height. She wasn't about to let anyone see that righteousness and courage were being rapidly replaced by a gut feeling that she'd made a colossal fool of herself.

"Obviously, they are engaged in some illegal and nefarious activity, or why would the man go through the trouble of dropping off a package every night to be picked up by the woman in a different car? I've seen her do that several times. It's even been stolen by a coyote a few times, so it obviously has developed an addiction to the stuff in there."

More laughter.

"I hope he's addicted to the stuff in there!" the man gasped between laughs.

"I'll take that comment as a 'no,' you don't know who this is," another trooper said, chuckling. "This is Dr. Brian Cooper, a nationally known biologist who is currently living in Silver Point with his wife, Vivian" – the trooper indicated the woman, who gave Maude a friendly nod – "and they are studying the adaptability of desert wildlife that have been in captivity and are again living in the wild, specifically, former pets and rehabilitated wildlife that are back in their natural habitat."

"Oh." Maude felt about two feet high.

"Except for the coyote, who is actually more like a dog," Dr. Cooper said. "He was raised by humans from a pup and spent about three years in captivity. The owner died, and a relative turned him into our wildlife rescue so he could be taught to live like his wild peers. Unfortunately, he did not readjust as well as we'd hoped, so, instead of taking him back to live with humans, we decided to provide food for him so he would not starve. Since we've started doing that, he has been able to stay away from humans and live on his own. He does well, except for the food. He never learned to hunt properly, for some reason."

"Why would he?" Maude asked. "Every day, he got enough food without having to hunt for it, so he now would expect that. Which reminds me, Mrs. Cooper, I saw you pick up the package a few times shortly after it was dropped off. Why did you do that?"

Vivian spoke. "Usually, because I wanted to add something to it. My husband generally takes care of creating the coyote's meals, but sometimes he takes it before I tell him there's more. So I pick it up, add whatever leftovers or food I've made for him, and then bring it back. But he does hunt a little. I've seen him pounce on desert rodents a few times, but I've always gotten the impression it was more for play than survival." She looked at her husband.

Dr. Cooper sighed. "I believe Vivian is right. He just does not see other creatures as prey. I'm beginning to think we should catch him and let him live with humans again. But it would have to be someone special, someone, with love for the desert and wildlife, who would let him be himself."

"Well, he certainly had no fear of me," Maude shuddered, remembering that watch kept on a moonless night.

Suddenly her hand flew to her mouth.

"OH?" everyone chorused, looking at her intently.

"I mean – that is, I mean, having seen him remove the package a few times, he doesn't seem to be the type of dog – uh, coyote, who is afraid of people!"

Her recovery was not the best.

"It seems to me, ma'am, that you are the one who should be arrested, not the Coopers." One of the policemen opened a notebook. "Unless you can provide us all with a very good explanation of your own 'nefarious' activities, we could rightly arrest you for stalking this couple and possibly trespassing on federal land." He looked at her sternly.

Maude wondered how she remained standing on two pillars of water. How her own activities had been viewed by the other people involved had never entered her mind. She felt she was in a boatload of trouble, and from her knowledge of cops and robbers on television, the best way out was complete truth. So she told it. All of it, from the first time her curiosity was piqued to the decision to make a citizen's arrest, which is how everyone got to have a good laugh at her expense this evening. She truly realized the trouble she was in with the law and began to mentally prepare herself for life behind bars.

"Well, that's it," she said sadly, as her tale ended. "I've told you the whole truth from my perspective, and I'm very sorry for the trouble I've caused you." She looked at the Coopers, who were now standing with arms around each other. "I'm too curious about things, and sometimes I don't think before I act. In this case, I thought too much. I'm very sorry. Can you forgive me? And will you visit me in jail? I'd like to learn more about what you do. It sounds so interesting."

The Coopers looked at each other.

"Well, anyone who would go through the trouble you have in trying to do the right thing shouldn't be locked up. You did it from your heart as well as your head." Dr. Cooper came and placed his hands gently on Maude's arms. "Yes, we can forgive you. And you're not going to jail, because I'm not pressing any charges. Officers, I'm sorry to have you come out for nothing tonight. I think this lady can go home in peace this evening."

"*Or in pieces,*" Maude thought.

"Dr. Cooper, we're not sorry," the third officer said. "It's good to know we have honest people around us who try to do right. We see too many of the other kind." They shook hands with everyone and departed.

Vivian asked a very humble Maude, "Did you mean that? Are you really interested in what we do, even though you weren't aware of our existence before tonight?"

"Yes. I grew up here. I've always found this area fascinating. I've gotten into more trouble regarding the desert and its inhabitants than I can remember. From small on, I was always bringing something home, alive or dead. I have this tremendous curiosity that needs to be satisfied, which is why I…went…rather overboard where you are concerned. It's just something in me. I can't seem to stop once I get curious about something. I just have to learn everything about it. Only, this time…." Maude lowered her head and sighed. "If you'll excuse me, I think I'll crawl home now. And thank you so much for not putting me in jail. I don't know if I can say the same were it the other way around." She turned to leave, then looked back. "Best of luck to you with this project. If I see any more packages, I'll look the other way and move into the far lane."

"Call me." Dr. Cooper handed her his card. "I may have a project you can get your total curiosity into. If you decide you have the time and dedication to do it – and it will take both – I'd certainly like you on my team."

Maude was floored and humbled even more. "Thank you," she said simply, taking the card. The Coopers watched her walk slowly to her car, head down. Dr. Cooper, seeing Vivian's vehicle right behind Maude's, got into his and pulled forward so she could get out.

"What are you thinking, dear?" Vivian asked as he returned to her.

"I'm thinking about Ivan."

Vivian was silent for a moment, then she knowingly said, "Ah," as the realization came to her. "Yes, I think she would work well with him. If she gets into trouble, Ivan can protect her – from herself, if need be!"

"You know me so well, dear." They kissed. "Go home. I think I'd like to study human biology later tonight."

"Mmm. I'll be waiting. I assume you're going to wait until the coyote shows up?"

"I think so. I don't know why he's not here yet."

"Would you come around with all these noisy people and lights here?"

"No. See you later."

They kissed again, and Vivian left, leaving Brian to his thoughts and the coyote.

Maude was very embarrassed, so for the next several days, she had no trouble minding her own business. Moe, Daisie, Herb, and her fellow employees wondered what happened. This was too unlike her. *Must have been something serious*, Herb thought and wished that she would not keep her own counsel this time. Mostly, he was content to let her do her thing, knowing he'd most likely have to rescue her, but this time she didn't need rescuing – his wife needed space and time. Sooner or later, he'd find out. Sooner, he hoped. But she remained silent.

While at lunch two weeks after the incident, Maude called Dr. Cooper's office. He was out but returned her call while she was in Quin's Gap picking up mail.

"Sure, you can come over after work. I'll be here late tonight, and we can talk about the project. You can find the place, right?

"Yes. I'll see you later."

That night, Dr. Cooper outlined his thoughts to her over coffee in his office. It was large, filled with papers, books, and magazines. Maude had to remove a stack of them before she could sit on the only other chair in the room. She listened intently as he spoke. Caring for desert wildlife certainly would be something she would love to do, and she was willing to give it a try. Never one to worry about what others thought, this time she had some concerns. Dr. Cooper reassured her that there would be no problems. He would be on call for her 24/7 as she and Ivan learned to work together. Yes, he could be difficult sometimes, but he felt sure she had the skills necessary for a good collaboration.

"Don't forget, this is on-the-job training," he reminded her. "You'll have two to three weeks of it while getting to know each other. Ivan used to be chatty, but he's pretty much stopped that. However, if he likes you well enough, he may start again."

"Not a problem, Dr. Cooper. When Daisie and I get together, the dictionary runs out of words."

Dr. Cooper chuckled. "When can you start?"

"This is evenings only at first, right? I don't want to get in trouble with my other job."

"Evenings only until the two of you are comfortable with each other. Then we'll see how things work out full-time."

"It'll be strange, not driving every day. You sure I can quit my post office job?"

"If you work for me, you'll have to. Maude, you have the determination to see things through. I need that in my employees. You'll be well compensated for your efforts. If you're uncertain, can you take a leave of absence until you know for sure?"

"I'll take a leave of absence, but I'm pretty sure right now. That lesson I learned from you a couple of weeks ago put a damper on my usual energy, but if you say I can handle it, then that's good enough for me. Two weeks ago, I would have jumped right in. But I've learned some humility, and now I don't just jump into the pool before making sure there's water in it. Don't worry, I swim like a fish." Maude grinned and put out her hand. "Let's do it. I'll start tomorrow night."

"Excellent!" Dr. Cooper's face lit up as he jumped to his feet and grasped Maude's hand. "I'll get everything ready. Just remember that even though many of these animals we work with experienced domestication, they are still wild. That makes them unpredictable. Ivan has helped in the transitioning of several animals from tame back to where they can function in their natural surroundings. You loved to roam the desert and care for its wildlife since you were a child. That is why I'm pairing the two of you. If you and Ivan are compatible, and strongly believe you are, both of you will work together with us to continue rehabilitation. So I'll see you at – what? – six tomorrow?"

"Six it is. I'm beginning to feel like my old self. And that's good!"

They hugged. Maude drove home, humming a tune.

All she told Herb was that she'd taken another job and would be working from six to nine or ten for the next three weeks and then going full time. Herb smiled and congratulated her. He knew he'd find out before three weeks was up what the new job was.

All he learned was that she was working on a project with someone named Ivan.

Three weeks later, Dr. Cooper called Maude into his office and motioned for her to have a seat. There was a large grin on his face.

"Maude, I'm very pleased with you and Ivan. You've learned to work together very well. He likes you, and I can see you like him. That's excellent. Are you ready to start your rehabilitation projects in earnest tomorrow?"

"I'm ready if Ivan is."

"He is. This morning, I found him standing in front of a cage containing a desert tortoise that someone kept for several years. That individual passed away, and the family dropped the tortoise off sometime during the night. They left a note indicating age and diet, so that's very helpful. We have started acclimating him to our facility today, and you and Ivan can start working with him tomorrow. Ah - there is one thing." Dr. Cooper paused. Maude looked at him.

"I've been thinking about your house and the property you have. Would you be willing to have Ivan live with you and Herb? He is homeless, you know."

"Homeless!?" Maude exclaimed, and thought for a moment.

"I'd be happy to have Ivan live with us! He and Herb will get along famously. He can have the spare room next to the garage. If he gets claustrophobic, there are a couple of acres of fenced-in land to explore. He will have plenty of places and critters to check out."

"Excellent! He has few belongings, so there should be no problem there. Let's tell him he has a new place to live."

Upon her arrival home that evening, Maude opened the front door and calmly walked in carrying blankets and a backpack containing dishes, following a coyote on a leash.

Herb's eyebrows shot up.

Maude shrugged and gave him a crooked grin.

"Herb, meet Ivan. Ivan, meet Herb," she said, as they walked through to the kitchen. "He'll be living here permanently, so get to know him. He's really cool."

Herb took a very deep breath and shook his spinning head slowly, continuing to stare as they disappeared into Ivan's new room.

Mistaken Identity

Sola, his hands pressed to his face, staggered blindly about, screaming. One moment his eyes had been staring at the Eiffel Tower, and in the next, he was trying to deal with the severe unexpected pain in both eyes. On a scale of one to ten, he would have rated the pain at thirteen.

Around him was chaos. One bystander screamed for the police. Another called for a doctor. Someone threw water in his face, hoping it would reach his eyes. Some people were on their cell phones, anxiously attempting to get through to whomever. A couple of men and a woman engaged in a heated argument, and in the distance could be heard the familiar "wee-ooo" of a siren. Another man and woman managed to grab hold of Sola and lead him to a bench, where the man pressed a wet towel to Sola's now swelling face. Another "wee-ooo" indicated the pending arrival of the ambulance. Police whistles pierced the crowd, which backed off a bit to allow them entry. Sola's anguished crying and coughing added to the cacophony.

The man and the woman helping Sola spoke urgently to men in white, who had appeared with a stretcher. The arguing group spoke to the police, as did a number of the bystanders—all at once, and in several languages. Sola was placed on the stretcher, which disappeared into the ambulance along with the two who helped him. The police were left to sort out what happened.

Although it took only a few minutes to reach the hospital, to Sola, it seemed like hours. His knowledge of French was minimal, but he did manage to understand that blinking his eyes rapidly reduced the pain. Oxygen helped him breathe easier. The paramedic in the ambulance got his name and some information and then questioned the man and woman, a married couple from the United States. Neither was sure exactly what had transpired, but they vehemently disputed a charge by the woman in the arguing trio that Sola had attacked her.

The ER doctor's examination revealed that his patient's eyes and face were reacting to pepper spray. The doctor called pediatrics and, within a couple of minutes, was applying baby shampoo to the affected areas. Sola's breathing became much better; the swelling also diminished. He left Sola with the nurse and went to the waiting room to speak with the couple who accompanied him.

As the doctor was getting information, the police arrived to arrest his patient. Their demeanor was apologetic. They really did not wish to arrest Sola, but the woman pressing charges was a high-ranking foreign diplomat who was threatening all sorts of political mayhem, and they explained they had no choice. The fact that it was a very warm day and Sola had chosen to wear a bit of gold jewelry and only his native loincloth didn't help his chances.

"But Sola is innocent!" the woman, Adrienne, exclaimed. "We were right behind him. My husband was reviewing his notes about the Eiffel Tower as we walked, so we briefly stopped in order for him to see them better, and within those few moments, everything went crazy."

"Did you see Sola touch the diplomat in any way?"

Adrienne replied, "I looked up in time to see the woman who was coming toward him appear to lose her balance and bump into him. Sola jumped and reached out to balance himself, and then he started screaming, his hands over his eyes. He may have touched her momentarily, but there was no way for him to have 'attacked' her! He's tall and muscular, but he's just a kid – he's only seventeen! He did not hurt that woman!"

At that moment, loud voices emanated from Sola's room, French from the nurse and strange syllables from Sola.

"What the…?" the doctor exclaimed. The entire group hurried into the room.

The ER physician was used to a multitude of languages, but this was incomprehensible gibberish to him.

He grabbed a wall phone. "Get a translator down here now!" he shouted into it.

"No need," Adrienne's husband, Frank, said. He stepped to Sola's bed, took the young man's hand in his, and began speaking the same gibberish in soothing tones. Sola grabbed Frank's arm, and they began an earnest conversation, the young man staring at Frank with his large round eyes.

"Do you know what they're speaking?" the doctor asked Adrienne.

"Esperanto. It's a contrived language that enjoyed great popularity around the world many years ago, although it never really caught on the way Spanish or Chinese has. In Sola's case, he learned it from his grandfather, and they used to talk with each other daily. I'm quite proficient in it, as is my husband, who's a language professor at a large university in the States."

Frank turned to the doctor. "It's okay. Sola just doesn't understand what's happening to him, and he's scared. He says he's fine and wants to get out of here. Can we leave now?"

The doctor thought for a moment. "No. Not before I make sure he's 'fine.'" He was adamant. "Everybody except you" - he indicated Frank – "out! I need to examine my patient. Nurse, escort the police and this lady back to the waiting area. I'll be with you shortly."

"*Messieurs, madame, si'l vous plait.*" The nurse firmly ushered Adrienne and the two policemen out of the room. The gendarmes continued to question Adrienne while they waited.

"Shortly" turned out to be over an hour. The police became agitated, not expecting to have this long a wait, and their fussing with the nurses at the station to hurry things up were met with aggravating apologies that there was nothing that could be done until the doctor gave orders, and he hadn't as yet. Adrienne was worried. She didn't believe anything was seriously wrong, but why this delay? Sola's life had been bad enough before she and Frank took him under their wings two years ago. Impoverished South American tribes don't have anything to offer their children except poverty and the misery that goes with it. As she stared out the doorway of the waiting area, watching other doctors and staff go in and out of Sola's room, she remembered the day they met him. Not having had a vacation in several years, they decided South America seemed an exciting place to take it. Going wherever they pleased, one day she and Frank rented a guide and a boat and chugged up a river to see the scenery and interact with native peoples. When they finally came ashore at a village to rest and stretch, Sola and his grandfather had been the first ones to greet them. Then a lanky kid of fifteen, he exhibited an intelligence that Frank recognized as exceptional. After discussing an idea with Adrienne, they returned to the village several more times. Long, friendly conversations with the boy's family and a number of gifts resulted in his returning to the United States with them so he could get an education and develop the talents the young man exhibited. Sola's desire was to use that knowledge to go back and help his people, and he turned out to be a very dry sponge, absorbing an ocean of knowledge rapidly and thoroughly. Their vacation in France was a gift from them to their protégé, a reward for his hard work, and a needed break from his studies. How in the world could it have gone so wrong?

The chief of police arrived. He begged, cajoled, ranted, threatened everyone with arrest, but nothing swayed the hospital staff. As long as Sola was under a doctor's care, he could not be arrested. In fact, he was being admitted. The doctor ordered a CAT scan to rule out a brain tumor.

Adrienne was shocked. Sola had never shown any type of abnormal behavior, unless you could consider a transplanted teen's fumbles while adapting to a completely new society "abnormal." The police left, dismayed, worried about what their government would do to them for not arresting the boy. They did not want to fight with this particular diplomat. During her career, there had been more than a few incidents leaving lives in shambles.

Fortunately for Frank and Adrienne, they did not know this, nor would they have cared if they had. Their concern was Sola. This boy was innocent of the charges, and Frank was prepared to move heaven and earth to defend him. Having the assistance of the US and South American consulates was particularly helpful.

They stayed with Sola overnight. The rising sun ushered in not only the morning but a top dignitary from Sola's South American country as well. After consulting with the doctor, the dignitary assured them that all would be well, and by that evening, they would be free to continue their vacation uninterrupted. The pretty young nurses were delighted that such a nice, intelligent, cute boy would be there all day, and they made the most of it. Sola, on his part, basked in the attention and asked a multitude of questions, absorbing all the information the staff gave him. Frank translated.

Late that afternoon, a semi-formal hearing took place in a meeting room at the hospital. Present were Sola in a wheelchair, Frank, Adrienne, the doctor and several colleagues, the US consulate, the South American dignitary, a judge representing France, and a representative of the diplomat, who had declined to appear, indicating the previous day's event was too traumatic. The representative spoke first, stating in explicit detail how Sola had moved in front of the diplomat, blocking her way, and expressing in unmistakable body language how desirable he found her and what his intentions were. Naturally, she needed to protect herself from these unwanted actions and used pepper spray in her defense. To prove her allegations, he showed the assembly a picture of a large bruise on her lower left arm where the young man allegedly had grabbed her. Adrienne gasped, and Frank squeezed her hand. The diplomat was willing to drop the charges, as she believed the boy's family had the resources to pay her for her pain and suffering.

Adrienne stiffened in outrage, but Frank only smiled. He and the South American dignitary exchanged knowing glances. The judge dismissed the representative, who smugly seated himself with the others. He had done this before, Frank decided, and turned his attention back to the trial.

Next to speak was the dignitary from South America. Following him were the ER physician and the doctor who interpreted the CAT scan. A psychologist and ophthalmologist also spoke. Frank gave his testimony, and by the time the American consulate finished with a counter-motion to sue the diplomat on false charges of sexual assault, the representative was sweating profusely. The judge indicated extreme annoyance with both her and her representative and determined that France, which normally held indiscretions with a *comme ci, comme ca* attitude, would conduct a thorough investigation of her previous cases. The rep did not relish going back to the diplomat and telling her that not only had she lost her case, her entire history of extortion was about to be made very public. Sola was declared innocent, and he and his American family were now free to resume their vacation.

Frank caught up with the diplomat's representative in the hospital café, where he was drinking some much-needed coffee and trying to decide the best way to flee the country while keeping his diplomatic immunity. Frank got himself a cup and joined the representative, who was still looking rather green.

"I'm sorry about your diplomat. She's not very diplomatic, is she?"

"Non, Monsieur! She is, how do you say, *tres difficile.* I was with her yesterday, and we had no idea who this boy is. He seems so – how you say – primal."

"Yeah, well, looks are deceiving. You'd never guess his uncle is the top diplomat for foreign relations for his country, would you?"

"Never, Monsieur! I don't know who you are, but you seem to have many strings you can pull also."

Frank sipped the coffee. "I do not use them unless absolutely necessary, but being a distant relative of said dignitary also helps."

"I do not relish telling Madame of the outcome of this trial. That CAT scan, those doctors – ai! Especially the one for the eyes." The representative bowed his head, hands over his own.

Frank stood, finished the coffee, and placed a comforting hand on the man's shoulders. "Yeah, well, Madame needs to know about that, doesn't she?"

The representative looked at Frank. "She will be mortified, as am I. There is no possible way Madame's claims can stand up. I am sorry for you, Monsieur. Your boy's affliction. He was by himself, head up, eyes on the tower. There was no indication."

"There wouldn't be. Sola's jungle training serves him well. He uses his ears and body to sense what's around him. If Madame ever again wishes to choose another victim," – Frank paused – "tell her to pick one who isn't totally blind."

Morgue

Hi. My name is Dave. I work the graveyard shift at the hospital morgue. Why the graveyard shift? Death can't tell time.

This hospital is busy 24/7. We serve not only a large metropolitan area but the county as well, even though we're not a county facility. Seems to me the county coroner should have his office with the rest of the politicians, but a decision was made a long time ago that he should be here. I pass his office almost every night.

Almost every night, did I say? Yep. Get one night a week off. I got hired years ago and know this job like the back of my hand. It's a good job for someone who tends to be a loner. Sometimes there's lots of activity, like when a couple of gangs decide to shoot it out, and sometimes it's very quiet. I prefer quiet. Never had a wife or kids, so my time is mine to do with as I please. Since no one wants to work my shift – the hospital tried hard to get someone after my coworker had a chilling experience a couple of years ago, but no luck – so I just stayed on alone. But I'm not always alone.

Lemme tell you about the chilling experience. It was summer, and the morgue was kinda busy that night. Couple gang shootings, a drive-by, and the hospital itself had a fire. Seems some idiot visiting a patient on oxygen lit a cigarette with a match in the patient's room, totally disregarding the "NO SMOKING" signs plastered all over. There was a hot time in the old town that night, let me tell you. Several people died. It was my night off, but I happened to be in the hospital on personal business when everything exploded around me. Barely escaped with my life. Ever since that night, Al refused to work the night shift. Our boss, Frank, said he'd seen a ghost. That musta scared all potential applicants, because from that time on, I worked the shift alone. Since I'd been here for twenty-eight years, I figured I could handle it by myself. The morgue was kept lit even if there was no one on duty, because, as I said earlier, death can't tell time. No point in keeping a body around to frighten other patients, and if they died in the emergency room, bodies were transported here immediately to make room for whoever needed the bed next.

I dunno about ghosts, but I'll tell ya another reason why I like to work nights: I discovered I could talk to spirits. Now, I ain't into spiritualism as such, you understand, but I do believe in an afterlife, and I do believe that our bodies are just vessels being used by spirits who inhabit the earth for whatever their reasons are. I've attended lots of lectures by ghost hunters, who said that sometimes spirits get so attached to a person, place, or thing that they get stuck here, and it takes a special clairvoyant to communicate with the person to help him cross over to the other side. Until that fire, I didn't know I was that kind of person.

I found out the night after. As I said, I was off, so I didn't have to come in until the next evening. By that time, the bodies of those who had been killed in the explosion or fire had been identified and removed to mortuaries or crematories, so except for a couple of stiffs who had died on their own during the day, there was really no one around – except for a sad-looking mousy man who kept bending over one of the bodies. He must have taken the death hard because he kept telling it to wake up and get to the library.

"Hey, Bud," I said sympathetically, "You the next of kin? Need to identify him?" I knew it was a him because of the shoes sticking out from under the sheet. I walked over and pulled the sheet back so the man could see the face and almost fell over when I recognized Mr. Mousy lying on the table! I looked from one to the other and almost fainted. Mr. Mousy looked at me with mournful eyes. "Yes, that's me," he almost squeaked. "I can't understand why I'm here. I should be at the International Librarians' Convention at the Hilton."

Well, as I said before, I believe in spirits, but until then, I ain't never seen one. I guess going to those ghost hunter lectures finally rubbed off on me. He didn't seem anything to be afraid of, so I invited him to sit down and talk about it. I looked at the tag on the arm. "Hit and run," it read. I shook my head.

Putting on my best Ghost Hunter air, I said, "Do you remember anything about going to the convention?"

"Why, yes, I do," Mr. Mousy said thoughtfully. "I remember that I was late because my wife became ill and I had to go home to attend to her. I drove quickly back downtown and parked the car myself instead of having the valet do it. I guess I should have let him park it because when I ran from the parking lot across the driveway to the hotel, some moron sped right into me and kept going. I must have been knocked unconscious because when I came to, there was a lot of commotion. Imagine my surprise when I saw myself being taken into an ambulance! I remember climbing aboard and watching the paramedics try to jump my heart with their paddles. I also seemed to be quite bloody, which annoyed me, because I was wearing my best suit. I followed them and me into the emergency room, but they couldn't get me to wake up. Then they brought me here. I *must* get up! I'm to deliver the keynote address tonight!"

Poor guy. Here was a good chance for me to help this poor soul across into the next world. I'd seen enough lectures about it and read enough books about the paranormal to have an idea of how to do it.

"Sorry, Bud," I said sadly, "But – by the way, what's your name? I assume it ain't Bud."

"It certainly isn't. I am Mortimer Harold Jackson III."

"Well, Mr. Jackson, it's like this. You got clobbered by a hit-and-run driver. I hate to tell you this, but you're dead. You ain't going to get up and deliver no lecture tonight because no one except me, I guess, can see and hear you. Youse is a spirit that is sticking around this earth when you should have gone home to the Afterlife. Why would you want to stay here when there is so much better? Why are you so attached to Earth?"

Mortimer Harold Jackson III pulled himself up to his full five-feet-four height and snorted, "I beg your pardon! I am not dead! I am very much alive, but I seem to be caught in his horrible dream! I would really appreciate it if you would pinch me and wake me up. I must get to the Hilton!"

I was about to reply with some sensible rejoinder when there was a racket outside the door. One of the night security guards ushered in an ill-looking tearful lady who kept wrapping and unwrapping a handkerchief around her hands. He took her over to the table where her husband's body lay. She screamed when she saw him, gasped, "That's him!" and fell in a dead faint to the floor. Mr. Mortimer H. Jackson rushed to her side, uttering nonsense stuff like, "Oh, Martha, dearest, I'm here! Snookums, wake up!" and other phrases sugary enough to give the hearer diabetes. Without seeming to be aware of him, the guard waved smelling salts under Mrs. Jackson's nose, bringing her around. He helped her to her feet, and half carried her out of the room. Mr. Jackson stared after them unbelieving.

"I guess I am dead," he finally sighed. "But if I am, how come you can see and hear me?"

I told him about my interest in the Afterlife and in spirits. I also explained that I wanted to help him get to the other side, figuring that a librarian wouldn't have any vices and shouldn't have any trouble going up instead of down. The only thing I didn't know how to do was to get him a guide, which is what the ghost hunters and clairvoyants said was needed to get the spirit to the right place.

Mr. Jackson slumped into my chair, head in his hands. Neither of us said anything for a while, me because I was too busy trying to think up ways to get him out of my chair and onto a cloud with a harp, and he because he was thinking over his life. I knew he was doing that because his thoughts kept horning into mine. Oh, great, I thought. Not only am I a spirit-seer, now I'm a mind reader!

Finally, he whispered, "Poor Martha. Poor, poor Martha."

This had me stumped because Martha wasn't the one who got bumped off. Maybe he didn't leave any insurance.

"I should have listened to her when she tried to get me to go to church with her. Now I see that she was only concerned about my welfare, not trying to force me to accept a dogma totally against what I see now as boorish intellectualism. Now I'm gone, and there is no way to explain to her that I understand what she's been trying to tell me for years. She'll think I've gone to – well, the hot place down under, and I'm not referring to Australia. Is there any way to let her know I'm a ghost?'

"Well, there is one thing you can do," I suggested. "Go home. Live with her. Talk to her when she's unhappy or has a problem she can't figure out. Let her know you still love her by picking one of your garden roses and putting it by her place at the table. Maybe by doing that, you can atone for not believing her and will eventually cross over with her when she kicks the bucket. I know that spirits do that kind of thing from the other side, but since you're here and not there, I see no reason for you not to do it where you're at."

Mortimer Harold Jackson III looked at me gratefully. "Thank you," he said simply. "I shall. I MUST!" *He likes that word, **I thought.*** "Thank you so much -?"

"Dave," I said.

"Thank you, Dave. I'm coming, Snookums!" With that, MHJ disappeared through a wall.

Now it was my turn to collapse in my chair. I wasn't scared, just unbelieving. Here I was, a morgue clerk for almost thirty years, able to help dead people with their lives – or, rather, their afterlives. *Wow*, I thought. *Ain't that somethin'.* I could hardly wait for the next stiff, but at the same time, I was reluctant to try this again. Helping spirits was a big responsibility, and I wasn't sure I was up to it, especially since I didn't seem to know any guides, and there wasn't a big line of them falling all over themselves to get introduced. I decided maybe that was a fluke experience and to lay off the triple Bloody Marys for a while.

The next few nights were uneventful, and as time passed without any ghosts, I started to think more and more that it was a one-time deal and wouldn't happen again. Just as I began to get comfortable with that idea, the medics brought in a kid.

As I said earlier, I ain't married and don't have any of my own, but somewhere in my heart is a soft spot for them, especially the cute ones.

And this one was. She lay there with a peaceful look on her face, curly brown hair falling all over. She wore a hospital gown. I looked at the tag. "Amanda Jacobsen, age four. Cancer." Ugh. How somebody so little could get that ugly disease, I never could figure out.

"Lift me up, please," said a tiny voice at my side. I looked down and jumped. There was Amanda, in a lacy blouse and pleated jumper, looking up at me ever so sorrowfully. I wasn't sure I could pick up a ghost, but she lifted easily. She even felt kind of solid, which unnerved me.

She sat in my folded arm, and we looked down at her.

"I don't want to hurt Mommy," she sniffed.

Now I always thought kids were pure, you know, mostly because they haven't lived long enough to get into really nasty stuff, but there's always an exception. Take my cousin's kid – looks like an angel, but with horns. I wondered what Amanda's problem was.

"How's a pretty little thing like you going to hurt your mommy?" I wanted to know.

The child looked at me solemnly. "She will get sick now," she stated. "It will hurt a lot. I know, because I hurt a lot, and the treatment made me very sick. But I did it because I love my mommy. I didn't want to see her get sick."

This lost me, and she must have seen my blankness.

"Before I was born," Amanda explained, "I knew that the lady who became my mommy would get real sick and die before she was supposed to. She is supposed to help my daddy see a truth about himself, and she is the only one who can do it. If she died, he wouldn't learn what he was supposed to learn, so I decided that if I got sick instead of her, daddy could learn what he needed to know. So I took Mommy's cancer away from her. I didn't know I would die." She began to cry earnestly, hugging my neck, and sobbing juicily on my collar.

This blew me away. Here I thought I knew about spirits, and this kid was telling me something I'd not heard before. Somehow, I knew she was telling the truth, even though it seemed farfetched. Out of the mouth of babes, I decided.

I comforted her as best as I could. I'd seen kids in here before. The reaction of the parents wasn't pretty. Must be really hard to lose a child;

some parents became unhinged and never were right again after that. I knew that because about ten years ago, a little boy was hit by a car. The parents came in to identify him, and the mother went bananas. She came in two years later, but if I hadn't read the name on the tag, I'd have never known it was her. She sure had let herself go. The husband had been stoic, but he didn't do too well after that, either.

I took Amanda over to my desk and sat her down on it while I placed myself in my chair.

"All right, Amanda, let's have that one over again. You say you knew that your mommy would get sick."

"Uh-huh," she hiccupped.

"How did you know? You were born with a medical encyclopedia in your hand?"

She gave me a disdainful look. "My body didn't know because I was just borned. But *I* knew, because I've seen it in heaven."

Whoa. This kid was way beyond me. What an imagination! I decided to go along with her story.

"So if you saw Mommy's illness in Heaven, why do you want to stay here? Don't you think youse can be more effective in helping her from there?"

"She needs me." Amanda was very matter-of-fact.

"Kid, mostly it's the other way around," I said. "Kids need their parents, not the parents needing the kid. Your mommy's an adult. She has a husband, your daddy. They are supposed to lean on each other, help each other. Sure, you can help, give them moral support maybe, but adults are supposed to be strong under these circumstances."

Amanda was a smart-aleck. "Then why did I take Mommy's illness? How strong do you think she'd be if she were sick in bed and throwing up and hurting after getting a treatment to make her well?" Her eyes bored into mine.

I gave up. "Okay, you win," I said. After thinking for a moment, I added, "If you saw all this from Heaven like you said, wouldn't it be better if you were there? After all, you could only do so much here. From that vantage point, you'd have all the angels and your friends and relatives to help you, not to mention God, if there is one." (Never let it be said that I'm not open-minded.)

Amanda considered that "Yes. I see. Then I need to go back to where I came from. But how do I get there?"

Kids and their questions! I really wished I had an angel or a guide or even my almost-mother-in-law, rest her battleax soul. Then I had an idea.

"Do you remember what Heaven looked like before you were born?" I figured, since we were only talking four earth years here, the little spirit might have some kind of memory.

She sat straight and looked earnestly at the ceiling. After a moment, her face brightened, and she cried out, "I see Gramma! Gramma! Here I am!" She looked happily at me and again at the ceiling. "Oh, Gramma, I see you. Come and get me! Take me home!" Her arms reached out.

To my surprise, Amanda started to fade. I could have sworn I saw a heavy-set figure take the little girl in its arms and start to rise with her.

"Bye, Dave!" she called. "Thank you!" Amanda faded from sight. Good thing, too, because at that moment, her parents entered for a final look. Her mother was young and good-looking but seemed to be about a hundred. Her father was pale and drawn. Sorrow filled their beings, making them old and stooped. I felt really bad for them. They'd had a wonderful daughter. I wondered if I should say anything, but decided to keep my mouth shut when the mother fell over her daughter's body, sobbing. Tears ran from the father's eyes as well. I retreated and let them have their private moments.

That encounter shook me. As I said, I believe in an afterlife, but when you start naming specific places, that gets a little too close to home for me. I was reared in a strict Lutheran home, but rebelled as a teen – who doesn't? – and rejected much of the teaching I didn't understand anyway. Still, over the years, I wondered about God and how He could create us and then leave us here with this mess and still love us enough to want us to come home to Him and – oh, forget it. I'm getting a headache.

I was just getting over the Amanda incident when I met Samantha: tall, lithe, long straight golden hair down to her waist, almost. She looked nothing like the bloody mess lying on the table. She sat in my chair defiantly, short skirt revealing too long legs crossed at the knees. Her attitude said, "Oh, yeah?" but her eyes revealed fear. I looked at the tag. "Samantha Doe, twenty-two. Domestic incident."

I viewed the body. It didn't look like domestic to me; it was more like "Attila the Hun incident." Her face was beaten beyond recognition, and the body was cut in various places. One shoe was missing. I'd seen lots of these "domestic" incidents. This was one of the worse ones.

"What the *&@#% are you staring at?" Samantha's language, deliciously alto, contrasted with the neatness and trim of her spirit's clothing. I decided to be cool.

"I'm looking at a beautiful spirit that came from this messed-up body. You don't match your physical nature."

"That body was never any %@^&* good to me, anyway. I couldn't get through to myself that I was worth more than I thought I was."

Oops. Sounds like Freud resurrected. If it were, he sure looked a lot better as Samantha.

"By the way, who the *&%# are you?"

"Name's Dave," I said softly, trying not to stare into her eyes. "I'm the morgue clerk on the night shift."

"So, you get to see a lot of these things." Samantha unraveled her legs and leaped easily to her feet. "Not very pretty, am I?"

"That depends on which 'I' you are referring to."

Her eyes flashed. "ME, dumbhead, the one you're staring at!" She paced nervously, stopping once to view her mangled remains. "Hmph!" she snorted and spun to face me. "There's another dumbhead. *&^#@ fool!"

I've heard people refer to others derogatorily, but hardly ever refer to themselves that way. It was clear that Samantha had little, if any, regard for her physical self. Most people, even some of the crumbs I've known, had a lot more respect for themselves than she did.

I offered her my chair again. "Wanna talk about it?"

"Talk! What @#^*# good would that do!?" She sat, still angry.

"It might help youse get over your anger so's you could go home to a nice afterlife."

She stared, unbelieving. Then she burst into musical laughter. *If I'd been twenty years younger,* I thought.

"Dave, you're a trip!" Samantha chuckled. "You don't really believe in that sap, do you?"

"I seem to be talkin' to a part of it," I said mildly, raising an eyebrow.

That stopped her cold. She looked again at her remains, down at herself, then back at me. She had nothing to say, and I let her say it. I got busy recording the information for the hospital's records, wrote down info on another stiff the medics brought in right before her, and started doing some leftover filing. When I finally looked at her, Samantha was staring at the floor, sagged in the chair. All the energy had left her.

I got us both some coffee and sat on the desk. She took it without thanking me. It had occurred to me that spirits couldn't eat or drink physical food, but apparently, Sam didn't know that. She drank half of it right down and hunched over with her hands, cradling the cup.

"Stupid *+$@%," she said finally.

"I hope you ain't referrin' to you."

"No. It's that hulking half-wit I chose as a boyfriend I'm referring to. If he couldn't understand something, he'd get mad. If something went wrong, he'd get mad. If something happened that he didn't like or didn't agree with, he'd get mad. I could deal with it unless he added alcohol to his anger. Then he went out of control."

"And he was drinking tonight, obviously."

"Not just tonight—for days. He lost his job." Samantha looked at me earnestly. "I honestly thought I could help him. Underneath all the crud was a kind, talented person who had a lot of difficulties getting the talent out past the anger. I tried for a couple of years to get him to see that the problems he had could be fixed, that he didn't have to lead the kind of life he thought he did. It looks like I needed the same lesson." She looked at herself again, and a tear slid down her cheek.

"Samantha, sometimes no matter how hard we try, the person we want to help just can't accept it. It ain't your fault you couldn't get through." Now I was soundin' like Freud. "That goes for yourself, too. I've been studyin' spirits for years. Sometimes the part of us that knows more than the physical self just can't get through the intellect that society foists on us. We're told from small on to be smart, to develop our brains.

Well, the part of us that's spirit has brains, too, and if we're really smart, we'll listen to that side of us. The thing is, most people don't. Then they find themselves dead and wish they'd done something different with their lives, something that the part of us that is you know but can't get through to the physical. That's real sad, Samantha. I wish you could have done that. Maybe you wouldn't be dead now."

The tear gave way to a flood. Sam covered her face with one hand and let it all out. I offered her a paper towel that was on my desk. She drowned it before being able to get a grip.

"My parents warned me over and over about him. They recognized this part of me, but I couldn't see myself that way. I used my intellect only to deal with the world, and this is where it got me." She put her head down on the desk. "How could I be so dumb?"

"You ain't dumb, just ignorant. Ignorance can be fixed. Unfortunately, you'll have to come back and try again. Next time, pick a body that's more in touch with the spirit you." Geez. I sounded so intellectual!

"How can I tell my parents they were right, and I was wrong not to listen to them?" Her tear-stained face searched mine for answers. "And how – HOW – can I have them see me like this?" Her hand swept to her body. "Oh, God!" She buried her head in her hands and wept, her frame rocking and shaking.

"Well – maybe I can clean you up a bit before they get here," I said softly. "You expectin' them any time now?"

She was crying too hard to answer, but her head shook a no. I let her go on while I took another look at the mess that had been her. Then I shook my head. I hoped the police had the guy and would give him life at hard labor. He'd really done a job on her.

(It took me a couple of hours after she left to make her presentable to the mortuary. They'd take over from here to make her look human again. Well, maybe not. Closed casket for this lady. I felt like crying myself.)

A weight on my shoulder made me look. Samantha was peering down at herself between half-closed eyes. They were red and swollen from crying. If it was possible for a ghost to look as pale as a ghost, that was Sam. Her face reflected an inner turmoil that I could only guess the depth of. If I'd had a butcher knife, I could have sliced her misery, it was so thick. "Oh, God," she shuddered again and collapsed on my shoulder.

Now I ain't a big guy, but I'm not Don Knotts, either, Samantha was a good ten inches taller than me and spirit or not, she was a bit much to handle. I was surprised at her solidity. But I guess when youse deals with the spirit world, youse learns more than what the clairvoyants tell you.

"Samantha." A gentle voice came from the vicinity of the filing cabinet. I shifted Miss Legs and beheld a tall, good-looking gent looking like he'd just stepped out of an L.L. Bean catalog. The shirt and pants fitted him beautifully. He looked like I wanted to look thirty years ago. Sam raised her face slightly.

"What?" Her voice was dull.

"Remember me?"

Sam rubbed her eyes and pushed herself to her own feet instead of stepping on mine. She looked blankly at him. "No."

"Remember 'Skunky'?"

For a moment, her blank face remained that way. Then light dawned, and her jaw dropped.

"No *&#%@ way!" she exclaimed. "Skunky!? It is really you?" Her face lit up, and she squealed with joy as she flung herself into his arms. They hugged tightly for a long moment. Sam pushed away, gripping Skunky's arms at length to get a good look at him. Then she squealed again and threw herself into his arms once more. It was beginning to look like an old-fashioned movie.

"You grew up!" Sam cried when they finally parted.

"No, Samantha, but you just did. I've always been this way, even as your baby brother."

"Yeah," Sam sniffed, half laughing, half crying. "You always did seem like a tiny adult. Whenever I had to babysit you, it always seemed as if you were babysitting me!"

"I'm one of the few adults in God's kingdom," Skunky explained. "So, of course, even when I was a baby, I acted grown up because that's what I am." He grinned at her. Gregory Peck, move over.

"Dave, this is my little brother, Skunky – I mean, Solomon. We called him Skunky because he was born with black hair that had a white patch on one side. It never did get dark, did it?"

"No, but eventually, my hair would have turned white to match it if I'd lived long enough." He gave his sister another hug.

"Skunky died when he was four. Some childhood disease or other. I was eight. He was my world, and I couldn't understand why he had to die. Nobody could explain it to my satisfaction. I guess that's when I started to be rebellious."

"You were searching for love, Sam, real love like you'd learned came from your Creator. I came to show it to you, but I caught a nasty bug from one of Mom's guests. By the time our parents realized I was ill, it was too late. You knew who I was, and that's why my death was so hard on you. You wanted that love back, and our parents couldn't give it to you, nor could they explain what you wanted. No one could. So you searched high and low, and unfortunately, you searched too low. Mom and Dad were right about your boyfriend. You saw some of my traits in him, but he was too far gone for you to do anything with. The police are dealing with him now."

"Good!" I interrupted. "I hope he gets life at hard labor."

"I can't say," Skunky replied. "Sam, don't be so hard on yourself. You're not a bad person; you made some bad decisions. Our parents will be heartbroken, but once they come over to our side, they'll see the truth, just as you will soon."

"'Our?'" Samantha asked.

"Of course. I've come to take you home." Solomon looked kindly at me. "Thank you, Dave, for taking care of her. Mom and Dad should be here late tomorrow. They live in another state. I hope it won't be too hard on you having Sam's remains here until they can identify her."

"Used to it," I said. "I'll try to explain what happened."

"Don't waste your breath," Samantha said. "They won't get it."

"Come on, Sam, let's go. Despite what you think, you've grown into a lovely woman." Solomon's voice faded along with the two of them. I sat heavily in my chair. Geez. Dealing with spirits can be a real upper as well as a real downer. This couple was both.

After that, spirits appeared four, five, maybe six times a week. On the whole, I was able to help most of them cross over into a good spot. A few refused to go and departed for whatever place on Earth they needed to haunt. I hoped I'd never have to deal with anyone going down.

Then I met Ralph. He was big, heavy set, outspoken, and had a philosophy that was learned at the College of Archie Bunker. Coincidentally, he'd been a butcher, and his nickname was "Meathead," although he didn't seem terribly meatheaded.

I'd gone back to the morgue after a coffee break and found Ralph standing in the middle of the room, looking lost and confused. He spotted me and called out, "Hey, youse with the coffee, where in the woild am I?"

"In the hospital morgue," I replied, adding the city, county, and state for good measure. He grunted and wanted to know why he was there.

Oh, boy, I thought, *a real brain.* "Maybe because you're dead?"

"Dead? Oh, yeah." He scratched his ample front slowly as this concept registered. I waved him to an extra-large wheelchair and sat at my desk. "I guess I must be. That bulge over there is me."

I got up to check the tag on the bulge. "Ralph Cameron, age fifty-five, cardiac arrest."

"Want coffee?" I asked, just to be polite.

"Nah. Got a beer?"

"Sorry. Alcohol isn't permitted on hospital property."

"Oh, yeah," he said again and took another look at himself on the table. Then he slowly took in everything that was in the room, which wasn't much: my desk and chair, a row of filing cabinets, a few tables for bodies, a multi-compartmentalized refrigerator for stowing stiffs, and a bulletin board with several-year-old memos on it. He made a face.

"Gloomy in here."

"I like it. Most of the time it's quiet, which is nice. A person should have some peace and quiet every day. Keeps 'em sane."

"Oh, yeah." Ralph looked at himself again. "So, how'd I get here?"

"I was hoping you'd tell me. You were here when I came back from my coffee break."

"Oh, yeah." He scratched his head and screwed up his face trying to remember. "Well, last I can recall, me and the boys at the packing plant had finished up a hard day and was sittin' at Murphy's for some food and a beer, just to relax after a hard day, y'know?" I nodded. "Ever eat there? No? Well, ah – what's your name? – Dave. Dave, ya gotta try it sometime! Best steaks in the world! Broils 'em, see? Real juicy! Buys 'em from us, y'know? Gets good beer, too. Imports it from Ireland. So a bunch of us is sittin' around, gabbin', drinkin, and waitin' eagerly for our steaks. I like mine medium-rare, lotsa juice, smothered in mushrooms and onions, and about an inch thick! Eat 'em all the time. Well, there we was, just havin' a good time when all of a sudden I get this feeling like I been hit with a Mack truck, y'know? Boom, right in the chest! I remember the guys callin' 'Ralph, Ralph!' like I forgot my name, y'know? Then I hear somebody shout, 'Call a doctor!' Last thing I see is this big fat steak in front of my face, and then everything goes dark. When I wake up, I'm here." He looked at me. "That's all."

"What's the wife gonna say when she comes in here to identify you?"

"My ex don't give a *&^#@, but a couple of my buddies might come in. Yeah, here they are."

It was true. A medic ushered in two heavy-set bums in dirty T-shirts and trousers that looked like they'd seen a war. The Civil War. It seemed more like they'd been indulging in beer than cryin' in it. Still, they were proper. One crossed himself.

"Yeah, that's Ralph, all right. Poor guy. We're gonna miss him."

The medic took some information and ushered them out. The one who'd crossed himself made the same sign in Ralph's direction as they left.

Ralph brushed away a tear. "Jeez, that was thoughtful of him," he said. "Patrick was always a nice guy, though. Always thinking of others." He sniffed. "I'm gonna miss them, too."

Now here was a guy who needed my assistance if ever there was one. We talked for a long time. Ralph's life hadn't been too good – Hell's Angels for many years, a prison term, odd jobs, a marriage that went on the rocks – it wasn't until a few years ago that he got this job at the packing plant and straightened out.

I didn't know what kind of afterlife he was facing, but it had to be better than the one he'd had here. At least, that's what my training told me. I told him about my ability and what life was like on the other side, from what I'd seen of it. Ralph looked forward to getting there.

The door opened. A tall movie-star-type gentleman in a gray three-piece suit entered.

"Pardon me. I hope I'm not intruding. I'm looking for Ralph Cameron."

"That's me. Who might you be?"

"My friends call me Syl. I work as a guide to transport people from this dimension into the other. We received word that you had an unfortunate occurrence, so I thought I might find you here."

A guide! Just who I've been waiting to see!

I rose. "I'm Dave," I said, extending a hand. Then I wished I hadn't. I always thought spirits from the other dimension were warm and friendly. This guy seemed friendly enough, but the handshake was limp, and he felt clammy.

"Yes. Well, Dave, thank you for taking care of Ralph. There are just a couple of points I need to clarify before we cross over, so would you mind answering a couple of questions?"

"Fire away," Ralph replied confidently.

"Back in 1982, you were still riding with the Hell's Angels, were you not?" Ralph nodded. "I understand that you turned down a request from one of your *good* – meaning straight law-abiding, church-going friends – to help him find his runaway son. Is that correct?"

"Yeah, well, it was like this." Ralph squirmed. "Y'see, the boys and I was planning to meet a rival gang at the river for some fun and games, see? I kinda thought it up, and I figured out a plan to surprise 'em, see, and I thought at the time, jeez, what if the boys find out I'm helping somebody do good, see, so I pleaded a previous engagement and turned him down."

"And you are aware that because you did so, the boy was found murdered in a warehouse some five days later?"

Ralph looked down. "Yeah. That was real sad."

"It was." The Suit reviewed his notes. "You would have found him, Ralph, and brought him home. Your friend never forgave you for not helping, did he, even though there was the chance that you wouldn't have discovered where the boy was?"

Ralph continued to look at as much floor as he could see over his ample expanse. He said nothing.

"One more question. In 1986, there was a murder at a popular casino where your gang was visiting. It was one of the female poker dealers. I believe she got in your way?"

"She had no business being where she was!" Ralph shouted. "She shoulda kept her nose out of our business. Me and The Pirate were having a personal argument. She shoulda known better than to cross between us!"

"However, given the fact that things were rather hectic all around, and running between you was her only way to safety, how do you account for the fact that you killed her?"

"I didn't kill her! Not on purpose! She got in the way!"

"But you and the Pirate, as you say, were having a personal argument. How is it then that your gang and his were fighting and shooting the place up?"

Ralph got defensive. "When one of us is attacked, it's like attacking the whole gang. We all go to help each other."

"And you shoved your knife at the Pirate just as she made a break for safety." The Suit shook his head. "Bad timing, I'd say."

"Yeah? Well, you ain't got nothing to say about it, screwball. That was years ago, and I served my time. Now, are we goin' to the afterlife, or are you goin' to stay here and play 'This is Your Life' all night?"

I was shocked. This was the first time this had happened. The Suit didn't raise an eyelash. He merely looked at Ralph and said quietly, "No, I am not going to play 'This is Your Life' all night. We are going. Now. Come along." He took Ralph by the arm and began to lead him away.

I felt something was wrong. Very wrong. I don't know why, but for some reason, I began scrambling for something good, anything, that Ralph might have done in his life to counter the trouble The Suit brought up.

"Waitaminnit!" I cried. They stopped and turned to me. "Ralph, are you sorry you killed that woman? You sure seemed like you were when he brought it up just now!"

Ralph thought, "Yeah. I'm sorry. I really didn't mean to hurt her. It was just a gang thing, y' know?"

"And what about the boy and your friend?" I asked, rushing on. "Didn't you feel sorry that things turned out the way they did?"

"Listen," the Suit interrupted before Ralph had a chance to answer, "I don't like where this is going. Now we really must be getting on. I have a number of spirits to collect – I mean to usher in – tonight." He tapped his foot impatiently.

"Dave is right," Ralph said. "I think you're rushing me out of here. Yeah, I was sorry I didn't find the kid. Kenny and me had been friends for years, y' know? I shouldn't have turned him down. I see it now. Actually, I saw it a few years after the incident, after I got my job at the meatpacking place." He turned to the Suit. "I tried contacting Kenny after my life got straightened out, but couldn't find him. I guess he moved after that. I wanted to offer him anything I could to repair the friendship, but he wasn't no place to be found. Ever since then, I've tried to help people. I ain't no Goody Two Shoes, but I ain't Black Bart no more, either. Friends are valuable. They're worth the time and effort it takes to keep 'em. Wish I'd known that before I hurt Kenny so bad." Ralph looked sad and angry and contrite, all at the same time.

The Suit didn't like what was happening at all, but I just kept pressing the issue. "Didn't you tell me that you helped out a nun once?"

"Oh, yeah, I remember that. I was going home, see, and I saw this lady wrapped in a ton of black material waiting at a bus stop. She seemed anxious and waved to me, so I pulled over and asked what was wrong. Said she was going to miss her train if she didn't get to the station, and there was no bus in sight, so I told her to hop on and hang tight. Had my Harley then, see? So I barreled down the street a couple of miles to the station. She looked a little flushed when she got off, but she was there on time. Said she was a nun, which surprised me, 'cause I ain't had no dealin' with them dames before, see? Said she'd pray for me, too. I thanked her and roared off before any of them prayers could attach themselves to me. But I think about her once in a while and wonder how she's doin'."

"Do you believe in prayer?" I asked.

Ralph thought. "Dunno. They can't hurt and probably help. Y'know – maybe that's what helped me turn around. See, it happened like this: I was –"

The Suit interrupted angrily. "We don't have time for this! Come at once!" He grabbed Ralph's right arm and pulled hard. I grabbed his other arm and pulled just as hard the other direction. Ralph looked surprised, and then did something surprising – well, maybe not. He broke free from the Suit and landed a wallop that sent the guy sailing over a table, papers flying every which way. Now Ralph was mad. I could easily see what a formidable Hell's Angel he'd been, and I wouldn't have wanted to get him mad when he still rode with them.

"Listen, screwball. I ain't goin' with ya! Dave! You still wanna hear how I turned my life around?"

"Yes!" The Suit was still seeing stars. He wouldn't be getting up for a few minutes yet.

"I was at the same train station that I drove the nun to, waitin' for a buddy of mine I hadn't seen for a couple of years. He'd belonged to another Hell's Angels gang in another city. While I'm waitin', I'm browsing in the gift shop, and I see this little statue of a nun. Well, that got me to thinkin' about her, and I remember thinkin' hope she's doin' well. Nice lady. The train's arrival was announced, so I went out to the waiting area. Imagine my surprise when a straight guy comes up to me and says, 'Ralph Cameron! Youse is a sight for sore eyes,' or words to that effect. I didn't recognize him, so I politely say, 'Excuse me, but how did you get my moniker?' 'Ralph! Don't you know your old buddy Joe Scarpelli?' Well, you coulda knocked me over with a feather. We spent all night talkin', and it turns out he had contact with the same nun! She talked him into goin' straight and becomin' a Jesus booster, and while I weren't interested in no church, when I heard all the good things that happened to him, I decided I'd had enough. I was broke, about to be thrown out of my apartment, and felt I couldn't go anywhere but up. So I asked him for some help getting' straightened out, and he helped me. That's another reason why I help others now. Or did. Somebody helped me when I really needed it, so I pass it on."

The Suit was beginning to come around, and I didn't like the look on his face. He was turnin' darker by the minute, and I needed to talk fast if I was going to save Ralph. The phrase 'and your sins shall be washed whiter than snow' or somethin' like popped into my head, so I asked Ralph if he was truly sorry for all the bad things he'd done in his life, and could he ask for forgiveness for them. Ralph thought for a moment, and said, "Yeah, if there's someone who could forgive me."

"There is!" I quickly explained what I'd learned when I was a kid. For some reason, all the things I needed to tell him came to me clearly, and I told him everything. Ralph's eyes bugged out. Then he lifted his hands to the ceiling and said, "If Youse can forgive Your people for all the bad things they did to You, please forgive me, too!"

"Can you forgive yourself!?" I cried.

"If somebody else can, I sure can!"

I'd like to say that there was the sound of heavenly harps and a cloud appeared to whisk Ralph to his eternal reward, but that didn't happen. Instead, the Suit let out a horrible cry that chilled both of us, and for a brief moment, he became his real ugly self. We both yelled and jumped behind my chair. He looked threatening for a minute, then screamed out again and vanished. We clutched each other, eyes closed, each doing our own form of praying. When I dared to look up, the room was normal, except for a smell like some garbage was burnin'.

"Phew! That was close!" I disengaged from Ralph's grip and stood up. He followed suit. If a spirit could be said to be white, that was him. I won't say he was shakin', but he weren't too steady.

"Now what?" he asked, plopping down in my chair.

I sat on the desk. "Dunno, but somethin's gotta happen. You can't stay here for the rest of your life. Oh. That's right. You ain't got a life. Looks like you got saved from the Suit, but where you're goin' now, I ain't sure."

"Geez, I wouldn't mind talkin' to that nun dame right about now," Ralph sighed. "Thinkin' 'bout it, she was real brave ridin' with me. Nobody 'cept another Angel woulda done that."

"That depends on the angel."

We spun. Standing a foot off the ground, lookin' saintly, was a tiny woman in a black dress.

"Sister!" Ralph cried. He jumped up, rush to her, and gave her a big hug. She was taken off guard but recovered quickly.

"Dave, that was the bravest thing you did tonight," she smiled, extricating herself from the grip of a grizzly.

"Sump'n was wrong, Sister, so I had to help Ralph. Somethin' told me the Suit wasn't who he said he was."

"The 'Suit,' as you call him, was exactly who he said he was – a guide, but he was a guide to the nether world, not mine. Hell is not a pleasant place, Ralph, and I really wish you hadn't told so many people to go there."

Ralph turned red. Sister chuckled.

"I think you should come with me. There's a nice place we'd like you to see. It's not the greatest piece of real estate, but it's not like a prison, and…" The voice and the spirits slowly faded from me. I sat down – well, collapsed is more like it – in my chair and looked around, half expecting to see a gallery of spectators. Why, I dunno. But I was alone. I was glad it was almost quitting time. I needed some sunshine after that experience.

I gathered my stuff and prepared to leave. My watch said two minutes to seven. I sat at the desk and thought about what had happened and about all the spirits I had talked to. I thought about the hospital fire that revealed my ability and how the room had exploded around me, blowing me out with the wall. Then it was seven. I grabbed my jacket and lunch bag and started for the door. Frank and Al came in, talking.

"Morning, Frank. Morning, Al," I said, going out.

"Morning, Dave," Al said, coming in.

Just before the door closed behind me, I heard Frank ask, "Why do you always say 'Good morning' to Dave as if he were here? You know he died in that hospital fire two years ago."

* * * * * * * *

Epilogue

Well, life plays funny tricks on us. It wasn't until I heard Frank say to Al that I had died that I realized that I was stuck here on the earth myself! I was the idiot who lit the match in the patient's room, even though oxygen signs were posted. I thought I knew more than I did. The resulting kaboom told me too late that I didn't. Then I realized that I could talk to all these spirits because I was one, too! What a shock! It coulda killed me, if I hadn't already been dead.

Then I got another surprise. All the time I was helping those spirits cross over, I'd been waiting for a guide. Guess what? I was the guide!! Since I'd studied all that paranormal stuff, I was in a good position to help the spirits. 'Course, some of 'em were real smart like me, see, and they didn't listen to me. So they ended up staying on Earth, haunting the place they died. Guess it's up to the next idiot to help them.

You'd never believe who helped me to cross over. Samantha! The week after I'd digested all this information about my own spirit-ness, she appeared to me outside the hospital. I still hung around there, hoping for someone to help me, I guess, and bingo! There she was. She helped me to see that I cut myself off from people because I'd been hurt a lot in former lives and really couldn't get close to anyone. That's why I didn't marry. Couldn't trust people. She told me that my "accident" was no accident, that it was my way of helping myself find my true home. If I hadn't helped those other spirits, she said, I truly would have been stuck in the morgue for the rest of my afterlife. Helping them was my key to healing myself of my lack of trust and finding the answers I needed to cross over. Ain't that a stitch!

Y'gotta excuse me. I'm getting used to my real home, now. A new spirit just arrived, and I need to assist him in finding his right place. Then I'm going over to Amanda's house and help her help her parents deal with the new kid they just had. After that, Sam and I are going to Disneyland. Hey, spirits gotta have fun, too!

It Came From Beneath the Bed

"**D**addy! Daddy!"

I ran screaming into the living room, where my parents sat watching television. Well, "sat" may not be exactly the right word, but I was all of five years old, so what did I know? I threw myself against his arm, tears streaking my face. Alarmed, he moved away from Mommy and swept me up.

"What?! What's the matter? Are you hurt? Did you fall out of bed?!"

"No, daddy, no! Help me! There's something under my bed!"

"OH!" He gave mommy a look, which she returned, and then held me close as we walked back to my bedroom, issuing comforting noises as we walked down the hall. He reached in and turned the light on, and I could have sworn something dark disappeared under the bed frame as we entered.

"Under there!" I cried, pointing to where the covers touched the floor.

Daddy put me down by the door. "You stay here," he said solemnly and tiptoed to the bed. He got down on his hands and knees and threw the covers up, shouting, "Come out, you monster!" Nothing did, and all was quiet, so he got up again.

"Come here, sweetheart," he coaxed, extending his arms to me. Hesitantly, I went to him. He picked me up and put me back into bed, saying, "Well, there was nothing under there, so I guess we scared him away. You don't have to be afraid anymore. The monster's gone."

I fervently hoped so as we kissed goodnight.

"Would you like me to leave the hall light on just in case?" Daddy asked as he left the room.

"Yes, please," I said.

"Goodnight, then," Daddy smiled as he disappeared down the hallway. I could hear him and mommy talking softly, and I assumed he was telling her how brave he had been to scare the monster away. I fell asleep, with thoughts of Daddy as a brave knight dissolving into dreams of princesses and knights and horses and other fun things.

This scenario was repeated at least once a week for the next year or so, with the monster appearing regularly on Tuesdays and/or Fridays. At first, my parents indulged me, but as time went on, their patience wore thin, and finally, after scolding, mocking, and then brushing me off as having too active an imagination, they refused to listen to me at all. If I tried to bring up the subject, they immediately changed it. I was going to have to deal with this alone. If it were my imagination, I didn't know how to stop it. If the monster were real, I'd have to stop him from coming through the floor. I decided to pour a big bottle of glue under my bed on the next night he came, thinking he'd get stuck in it on the other side of the rug.

But I didn't have to. The monster never returned. It took me a while to get used to being able to go to bed without being afraid, but once I did, bedtime stopped being a hassle. My parents complimented me on finally realizing that it was only my imagination, but I never was sure about that. It was too real to me.

Life went on, and I grew up, and one childhood game did become a reality: I became a policewoman. Five years after graduating from the Police Academy, I became a detective. Living in a large Midwestern city was not like being a detective on "Law and Order," my favorite show growing up, but it had its share of drugs and prostitutes and the seamier side of life. My parents, although proud of me, worried too, because they never knew when (or if) they would get a call that I had been the victim. I don't know why they worried about that; I was smart, gutsy, and fearless. On my own, I had furthered my study of martial arts and felt I could take down Texas Ranger Walker if need be.

Four years passed. I heard rumors of a promotion, but knowing how information can get skewed, I put it down as just a rumor. The ones on the street were rampant: I was a witch (the kind that used magic, although the other could be appropriate at times), I was a wildcat, I had sex with the guys regularly (yeah, sure), my boyfriend was Godzilla because he's the only one I couldn't beat, etc. The truth is, I like men, but not for multiple partners, and I was a softie where kids were concerned. Olivia Benson had been my favorite character, and I guess I modeled myself after her, but I felt I was tougher. A lot tougher. In this business, you close your heart to survive. Street reality is a rough reality. I've seen cops so hard, you could cut diamonds on them. Andy Griffith doesn't cut it in today's big city.

That particular day had been very difficult: a shootout, a bank robbery, a rape, a child abduction, and that was just the morning. By the end of the day, I had had it. REALLY had it. I kicked off my shoes and flopped backwards on the bed, breathing heavily. I loved my job, but some days shouldn't happen, and this had been one of them.

After a while, I forced myself to get up and change clothes, wondering aloud why I had ever chosen to become a cop. Was I nuts? What was going to happen to the child who'd been hit by a bullet during the shootout? What about the young woman who'd been raped? She couldn't have been more than fifteen.

The s.o.b. who did it hadn't been nice. Her bruises and cuts would heal, but the emotional scars – I made a mental note to call the hospital about both of them. The abducted child had been found unharmed at a gas station seventy miles away from her home. The afternoon – well, let's not go into that. Even tough ol' me had had my fill of man's inhumanity to man. Take a deep breath, girl – let it out slowly, let out all the exhaustion, disgust, anger, and frustration of the day. I had to do this several times before I felt human again.

I threw together a conglomeration of leftovers for supper and settled down to watch TV. Nothing seemed interesting as I channel flipped.

Bah, humbug. I turned it off and called the hospital. The kid was going to make it okay; the young woman was something else. Heavy sedatives had finally gotten her calm, but her parents were still giving the hospital a hard time. I momentarily felt sorry for all of them.

Frazzled again, I took a shower and put on my favorite nightgown, one with a baby chick wearing glasses. "Chick with brains," the logo read. At the moment, I felt mine were still somewhat fried.

The lights dim, I crawled into bed and propped myself up to read. I must have fallen deeply asleep because I kept hearing this bell ring in the distance. It rang for a long time before my brain processed the sound as the telephone. I finally reached for it.

"Parker here," I muttered.

"Alicia? Ted. I heard about the day you had. How are you doing?"

Ted was my sometime boyfriend, mostly friend. We'd graduated together and then got separated into different departments. We saw each other regularly, if regularly meant whenever our screwball schedules permitted it. He was a good guy, supportive when needed, disappearing when necessary. I liked him.

"What time is it? My eyes don't want to focus."

"Almost ten. Did you eat yet?"

I couldn't remember what I'd had, so I said not really.

"I'll bring Chinese. See you in twenty."

"I'm in bed."

I could see the grin. "Then you'll need company for sure. We can celebrate your thirtieth in a special way."

"See ya." Click. Buzz.

Oh, great. A day like today topped with a reminder that I was leaving my twenties and becoming an old lady of thirty. But maybe a sympathetic shoulder was what I needed. I splashed cold water on my face and ran a comb through my mostly unruly hair. *Maybe if I let it grow*, I thought.

The food was excellent, and Ted had even managed to get a quart of tea. He'd been right. Having company and good food worked wonders. I was actually feeling almost happy and sleepy enough to get some good rest by the time he said good night.

"Why leave so soon?" I wanted to know.

"Why leave at all?" he responded.

"Mmmm." Being in his arms and gently kissed felt wonderful. It reminded me for some reason of Daddy reassuring me about no monster. Now why in the world did I think of that?

"How about slipping out of your granny gown and into something more appropriate – like skin?" Ted whispered, his lips tickling my ear and sending quivers down my back.

"Give me five," I whispered back.

"Seconds?"

"*MINUTES*, silly." I squirmed out of his grasp and hurried to the bedroom. Now where had I put that nonsensical underwear the girlfriends had given me at graduation? In the back of my dresser somewhere....

The heavy breathing behind me sounded like Ted wasn't willing to wait even five minutes.

"Ted, I thought you were going to give me a couple of minutes."

The raspy reply froze me in mid-throw and gave me chills very unlike the ones I just experienced. My heart started to race, and I almost screamed for Daddy. I hadn't felt like this in years. What in the blazes..??

I turned slowly as if about to face a perp. Keeping my shaking to a minimum, I looked up and saw what I couldn't believe was true.

It was the Under the Bed Monster.

No. Couldn't be. The Chinese food must have been laced with some hallucinogenic. Get a grip, girl! You're about to be thirty in – I stole a glance at the clock – forty-nine minutes, and you've got a monster in your bedroom. Training took over, and I said in my best squeaky (drat!) voice, "W-w-whaat are you doing here?"

The monster sat on the bed, causing it to squeak almost as much as my voice.

"We need to talk. I need to talk. Er – one of us does." He looked a little disconcerted and, now that I'd had a chance to actually see him with grown-up eyes, not half as scary as he had been.

"About what? You scared the life out of me for a year and no one believed that you were real! If you're not real, how come I'm talking to you?" (He's not real, he's not real, he's not real…oh, please let him be not real!)

"Uh, no, actually, I have something important to tell you. It's about your-"

"Lish? What happened to your voice?" Ted came out of my bathroom, a towel wrapped around his waist.

I tried to lower my voice, but wasn't very successful; squeaks kept coming through. The fact that Ted couldn't see the monster wasn't helpful at all. Old feelings of dismay, helplessness, and panic surfaced, despite my efforts to be in control. Suddenly I was five years old again, the monster was in control, and no one believed me. I wanted to scream, to rush into Ted's arms crying and blubbering, "Save me!"

"It's all right, Ted, I think I'm suffering from the stress of the day."

"You were way more relaxed a few minutes ago. What's going on?"

"I'm sorry. Some memories came back." (Get out of here, Ted! Don't let me freak out in front of you!) I was shaky.

He came across the room and gave me a hug and a kiss. "Give me a few minutes in the shower, and I'll take aaalllll the stress and scares of the day away."

I smiled wanly and sank back against the dresser. "I'm waiting," I sighed.

Ted whacked me on the hip and disappeared. A moment later, we could hear the rush of the shower.

The monster watched the exchange with interest. "Do you play with him often?" he asked.

"Play-" Sex moves flashed through my mind, and then I realized that Monster didn't know anything about that. He thought like a child. "Oh, yes, sometimes we do." (Wait a minute, what business is that of yours what we do?!)

"He's a nice boy." Monster looked thoughtful. "Oh, yes, what I came to talk to you about is your childhood. You've lost it."

(I'm just minutes from thirty years old and talking to a monster in my bedroom? You bet I've lost it!)

"Do you know why I came to your room so often?"

I shook my head.

"Because you were such a beautiful child. I liked you a lot. Now you're a grownup, and you are still beautiful…on the outside."

"What do you mean, 'on the outside'?" My fear was being replaced by indignation and curiosity.

"When you were little, you were thoughtful and loving and did a lot of things for other people. Yes, you were only five years old, but do you remember the time your neighbor fell and hurt herself? When she came back from the hospital, you went to see her every day and sometimes took flowers from your garden. You gave another kid your favorite toy because he didn't have any. Your mother didn't have to ask you to help her very often – you just did. When your daddy became ill, you were the very solemn nurse who gave him his medicine every day and sat with him for a while after kindergarten, telling him what you learned that day and showing him your drawings. He really appreciated that. I just liked being near you because you had such beautiful energy. It made me feel better after being rejected all week by other kids. You were afraid of me because you didn't understand that I wasn't there to frighten you – I was there because you helped me, too, just by being you."

Thank goodness the shower was still going. "So, why are you here tonight?"

"To tell you that you've lost your childlikeness. Being a child sometimes and being like a child when you're grown up can be very healing. Your heart – when was the last time you did something for someone just because that person needed it?"

"I –" I tried to remember and couldn't. Even Ted did more things for me way more often than I did for him.

"If things were turned around," Monster continued, "would you have taken Chinese to Ted tonight or would you have done police work?"

"Well, work, of course."

"That's what I mean. Your work is your life. Your life should be your work. You fulfilled a childhood dream and became a policewoman, but it's killing you inside. I can see your heart, Alicia. It looks like last week's broken-up concrete. Once it was soft and loving; now –" He broke off with a stifled sob, which really took me aback.

The shower stopped. "Ready or not, I'm coming!" Ted called.

"I'm not ready!" I called back, not even thinking. What Monster said couldn't possibly be true! Could it? "I give my life for my community!" I shot at him. "What do you mean, my 'heart looks like last week's broken concrete?'"

"Think about it. You're giving your life for your community – literally. Your name is still Alicia, but you're not her anymore. The little girl I liked to be around is now a hard, could-care-less grownup. Your life is killing you, dear. Minute by minute, your heart grows harder. You shut people out more and more and think you're protecting yourself. You're not. You're building a wall around you. Pretty soon, it will be too hard and thick for anyone to get through – even Ted."

I just stared. How in the world could this figment of my imagination be telling me all this? I stood straight, facing him squarely. I could see steam coming from the bathroom. Monster also stood.

"Here comes Ted. I hope you can play nicely with him tonight. Don't forget to give him your favorite toy."

"I think you'd better leave," I said firmly.

"I am," Monster replied. "Goodbye, Alicia. I won't be seeing you again." He got down on his hands and knees and vanished under the bed.

I stood there staring, a mass of quivering emotions. Ted had emerged and stopped suddenly; his face was blank when I focused on him.

"If that's what you want," he said evenly. "I thought I was helping you out and could be a comfort to you tonight, but if you don't want me…"

"Yes! No! Oh, I don't know what I want!" I cried. He turned back to the bathroom, and I realized he'd heard me tell Monster to leave and thought I was telling him! I ran to him and grabbed him by the arm, pulling and turning him toward me. "Stay with me! I need you tonight!"

"No, Alicia. You are right when you say you don't know what you want." Ted continued to speak quietly and pulled free from my grasp. He grabbed his shirt and put it on. "You've changed. You're not the same girl

I used to know. I don't know who you are now." He pulled up his trousers and fastened the belt.

"You've allowed yourself to become hard. You work hard, but you don't play anymore, hard or otherwise. Your work is your life, and it's taking a big toll on you." He strode toward the door. "Think about it. When you've decided what and who you want in your life, let me know. Don't bother, I'll let myself out." He closed the door gently when he left.

I just stood there, devastated. Oh, that horrible monster! He ruined my night! *I hate you*, I thought, and then stopped dead. Oh, my God. I had never told a soul in my entire life, "I hate you." *I don't need you either, Ted*. I spun and stomped back into the bedroom. Throwing myself on the bed, I suddenly started to cry like the little girl I no longer was. "Daddy," I sobbed.

Things got rougher. If I thought the day had been bad, it was nothing like the night. The day had been spent dealing with other people's problems; the night was spent dealing with mine. By morning, I was a wreck. I called in sick and later called back to say I was taking a week off. Personal business. I was cold and impersonal over the phone.

My parents were surprised but pleased to see me when I showed up unannounced the following day. I spent the days doing woman things with Mom and the evenings talking life with Dad. I slept in my old room, half expecting Monster to show up. In fact, I wished he would. But he didn't.

At the end of the week, some decisions made, I checked my finances and decided I could take an unpaid leave of absence for a month. I faxed an off-work form to my boss, thoughtfully filled out by the old family doctor, citing stress as the cause. Well, it was semantics, but not entirely untrue.

The month was spent revisiting childhood haunts and friends. In the end, both my eyes and heart had been reopened.

I put in for and got a transfer to the juvenile unit. Heartbreaking? At times, yes, but those kids had an inner strength and resiliency that I, like many adults, had lost (fortunately, they were helping me retrieve mine). They taught me a lot, as I taught them that there was a better way to live than life had provided. My hours were more regular, and I had time off. Ted and I got back together and talked about marriage. He told me how happy he was that I'd rejoined the human race, and I hit him with a stuffed animal. One major tug-of-war and much laughter later, he popped the question. I couldn't turn him down. I was giving him his favorite toy.

I thought of Monster and wished I could invite him to the wedding. I remembered the night he visited me and gave me his message, thinking of why he came, enabling me now to see that I was becoming again the Alicia he knew. Thank you, Monster. You saved my life.

Was there a *monster* under my bed when I was five? You tell me. I don't know.

The Silver Plate

Ten-year-old Henry Smith waited impatiently on the corner for his friend. It wasn't like Perry to be late, especially not on the first day of summer vacation, when there were bikes to be ridden, woods to explore, and frogs to catch. Henry shaded his eyes, squinting down the shady street where Perry lived, hoping to catch sight of him. They lived around the block from each other, and Henry considered going back home into his back yard to climb the big elm that semi-blocked his view of Perry's house; from the crook of the first main branch of the trunk, he could see into his friend's bedroom, and they had exchanged many a secret message from that position. But then, four houses down, Perry shot out of his front yard on his bike, skidding to a halt next to Henry.

"How come you're late?" Henry asked, grabbing his own bike and jumping on.

"I'll tell you later. Come on, let's go." He sounded annoyed, also not like him.

They pedaled hard up the road from their houses to the lane leading to the woods, Henry trailing several feet behind. He was slightly overweight, preferring eating to other forms of exercise, but usually, by the end of summer, he was as fit as Perry, who was slim and athletic. Henry found this hard to understand, Perry being the bookish one and he being one to play baseball, climb trees, and hike in the woods. But all that made him hungry, and Henry was always glad to get home and raid the well-stocked refrigerator. But once they had started their fun day, Henry forgot about food and concentrated on keeping up with Perry.

The boys rode off the pavement onto a dirt lane leading into a group of trees which was actually the very end of a pristine forest. Although a wooden slat fence separated the trees from the wild grasses and weeds leading to it, there was one section that was broken, and they pedaled through it, off the lane through the forest to a stream about a half a mile in. Perry braked and let his bike fall as he jumped off.

"The last one to the water is a tadpole," he shouted, leaping over a rock into the stream, shoes and all.

Henry was puffing. "Hey - wait! I've got jars!" His bike, complete with fenders and saddlebags, fell on Perry's as he dismounted. Opening a saddlebag, he pulled out two clean plastic peanut butter jars, perfect for small frogs, salamanders, or whatever other water creature was unlucky enough to be available for capture. They explored among the rocks and leaves along the shore, wading upstream until they had a salamander and two frogs each. A sunny clearing invited them to flop, which they did, removing wet sneakers and socks to dry them out.

Perry was in a much better mood. He watched his captives move around in the jar, contemplating what to do with them once they were home. Part of the basement of his house was set up as a wetlands diorama, and he had kept fish, insects, and frogs successfully for a couple of years. Although a year younger than Henry, he was in the same class, and they had been friends since first grade. Perry's bookishness was complemented by Henry's hands-on practicality, resulting in their working very well together, whether on a school project or, like today, just enjoying the outdoors catching wildlife.

Henry watched his friend. He wanted to know what had happened to make Perry upset and late, but hesitated to ask. Sooner or later, his friend would tell him, and he hoped it would be sooner.

The warm June sun felt good on their skins. Perry was lighter than Henry and subject to sunburn, but Henry had had his own share of blistered skin, so he was thinking about getting home when Perry asked, "What would you do if someone were moving into your house and you had to give up your room so that person had a place to stay?"

"Whoa! That's deep!" Henry exclaimed. He thought about it for a minute, then said, "I don't know. But I imagine I'd be pretty upset. Depends on who the person is, though."

"That's just it. I don't know. My dad and mom have been having some serious conversations lately, but they didn't tell me why until this morning. I think it's my dad's grandma or something. He called her 'GrandmaMA,' accenting the last syllable. I never heard of her before today. It seems she had some kind of accident and she has to come to my house to recuperate. We've got a big house, so I don't know why she has to have my room. There are other rooms she could have."

Henry thought again. "Well, you do have your own porch, and your room faces the sun in the morning. Also, you have your own bathroom." He glanced at Perry, who was looking glum again. "When is she coming?"

"Today or tomorrow. Why?"

"If it will make you feel better, I'll be with you when you meet her."

His friend lit up. "You will? Gee, thanks, Henry. Maybe if things get too bad, I can bunk at your house for a while."

"Sure. My parents won't mind. At least, I don't think they will."

"These jars are getting warm. We'd better go home."

The shoes and socks were still damp, so they waded back upstream and rode home barefoot, going to Henry's house first. Mrs. Smith greeted them and laid out glasses of milk and snacks while the boys went to Henry's room to deposit the jars. After eating, Henry put on dry socks and shoes and accompanied Perry back to his house.

The boy's worst fears were realized. Seated regally in a wheelchair in the front parlor was a frail, ancient woman, lap covered with a thick blanket, a lace sweater around her shoulders. White hair piled loosely on her head accented the bird-like features of her face. Deep-set dark eyes flashed intelligently as she studied the boys standing awkwardly in the doorway of the room. Perry's father, Anton LaFarge, sat beside her in an overstuffed chair. He smiled and beckoned them in.

"Grandmama, this is my son, Perry." He put an arm around the boy as Perry stood uncertainly beside him.

The old woman extended her hand. Perry shook it carefully, afraid of breaking the long bony fingers wrapped around his short, thin ones.

"Ah, so this is my great-grandson." Her voice was musical, if slightly dry. "Pierre. That was my husband's name." She momentarily transported to a different century, a different culture. Back again, she eyed Henry.

"This is my friend, Henry Smith. He lives around the corner from me." Perry spoke nervously.

Henry bowed slightly from the waist. "Pleased to meetcha," he said solemnly.

The old woman smiled. "*Enchanté*, young friend of Pierre's. We shall get along, no?"

"No, ma'am. I mean-yes, ma'am, I hope we shall." Henry wasn't used to formality.

Anton stood. "Henry, why don't you help Perry move some of his things to the room near the kitchen? I've already placed the rollaway bed in there and a dresser."

Perry groaned, receiving a stern look from his father. "Sure, Mr. LaFarge," Henry said cheerfully. "I'll be glad to help." Perry shot him a glance, which was ignored.

"Go on now. I will help Grandmama with her things."

"Wait!" the old woman commanded. She looked from one to the other. "Your son, he is giving up his room for me?"

"Yes," Anton replied. "We decided it was the best thing to do."

"But Dad," Perry wailed.

"Go," Mr. LaFarge commanded.

"Aw, geez."

The old woman caught his arm. "I will remember this kindness," she said quietly. There was something about her attitude that checked Perry's. He took a deep breath.

"Yes, ma'am." The boys went off to do the move.

"How long is she staying?" Henry whispered, even though from Perry's bedroom, they couldn't be heard in the living room.

"Forever, I guess." Perry resigned himself to the task. "Come on, let's get this stuff to my new room. Don't forget my frogs."

From the boy's point of view, things went from bad to worse. His parents catered to the new guest, and his father spoke a funny language to her. Perry avoided her as much as he politely could, but he had to admit she really wasn't all that bad. She asked the usual grown-up questions about school and his friends and hobbies, and spoke of her childhood, first in the country close to a city Perry had never heard of, then in the city. Curiosity got the better of him, so he looked it up in the world almanac. He found France easily enough but didn't find the city. Grandmama also spoke the funny language a lot, which his father said was French and translated for both him and his mother. He didn't understand it or why she didn't speak more English, though she seemed to know it well enough.

"I think she's senile," Perry complained to Henry a week later. "She talks about a silver plate a lot, even when she speaks English. It's 'silver plate' this and 'silver plate' that. And boy, is she bossy! My dad jumps when she says something. You'd think she was the queen or somebody."

"My parents said that a lot of times, old people get that way, especially if they're real old. I think she must be at least sixty."

"At least! I wish she'd go home again. My parents spend all their time with her. We haven't done anything together since she arrived."

Henry was properly sympathetic. "I'm sorry that she's there. Hey, my dad and I are going to the park tonight for some baseball practice. Why don't you come along?"

Perry lit up. "Yeah, sounds great!"

"Do you have to tell your folks?"

"Nah, they won't even miss me. Besides, if they know I'm with you, they don't worry."

"Great! Hey, let's go get some ice cream at the drug store."

Perry's evening did not go exactly as planned. He got home around nine to find his parents pacing the living room. When he hadn't shown up for supper, they assumed he was with Henry, but when it got dark, and he still hadn't come home, they began to really worry. They sat him down in the kitchen for a frank talk. Perry explained where he'd been and why he hadn't told them, and they explained back that even though the two families were good friends, it was still necessary for them to know where their child was. Mr. and Mrs. LaFarge hadn't realized Grandmama had taken up so much of their time and promised Perry a trip to the zoo as soon as they could find someone to stay with her for a day. Perry felt better then, even though he was grounded for two days.

Things didn't change too much at first. Grandmama still kept talking about her silver plate, and the LaFarges still catered to her, but now Perry was included in more of the conversations and activities. But then the boy noticed a tension in the house that gradually increased. His parents began arguing, something they seldom did, and even though they kept it quiet, he could hear the tone of their voices. It made him sad.

One warm night when he couldn't sleep, Perry heard another argument starting in the kitchen. This one had a different tone to it. He got up and opened his bedroom door a bit to hear better. His parents were discussing Grandmama's stay. Mrs. LaFarge felt the old woman was putting too much of a strain on them and wanted her to go to a residence, and Mr. LaFarge felt that since he was the only relative who lived anywhere near her, he should be responsible for her. After all, she was a hundred and two. Besides, where was the money to place her, even if they wanted to? He agreed that the prospect of her moving in permanently with them was one he did not relish, but she was too frail to go back to her old house and live alone again. The doctor said he was going to send a physical therapist to the house to help her walk, but even once she was walking, where could she go? What could they do with her? The discussion went in circles, ending with no real conclusion.

The next day, Perry got up for an early morning breakfast with his parents. He asked about Grandmama's house, and his father explained that she lived in an old mansion in the once elite part of town, now fallen into disrepair. The old money that had bought or built the homes was gone, and the new money built near the golf course or lake. Many of the homes were neglected because the old residents either had no resources to maintain them or the houses were unoccupied. Some had been for sale for a long time, but people weren't interested in hundred-year-old homes that needed extensive remodeling or repairs, as did Grandmama's. This is why Grandmama most likely would continue to live with them. It would be difficult, perhaps, but they would manage somehow.

"But what about her silver plate?" Perry asked. "Couldn't you sell that and get some money?"

The LaFarges looked at each other.

"What silver plate, dear?" Mrs. LaFarge wanted to know.

"Grandmama talks a lot about her silver plate, so I thought you knew about it."

His parents looked at each other again.

"No, son, we don't," Anton said. "I don't believe she's even mentioned that to us."

Perry looked confused. "Well, I've heard her mention it lots of times. But maybe her mind isn't working right."

Mr. LaFarge was surprised. "There is nothing wrong with her mind, son. I don't know where you got that idea."

Perry didn't answer right away. Then he asked, "Would it be all right if Henry and I rode our bikes to get a couple more frogs today? The ones I got last time both died."

"Sure. Just don't stay out after dark again without letting us know."

"Thanks, dad." Perry finished his breakfast and went to call Henry.

"I got two more jars," Henry said when they met an hour later.

"We won't need them. We're not going to the forest today. I got a plan." Perry related the earlier conversation with his parents. "We're going to Grandmama's house to find that plate. She needs the money."

"Wow," Henry breathed. "Do you know where her house is?"

"Not exactly, but I have the address from a piece of mail that was forwarded to us. We could ask somebody when we get there. We're going to need a large sack and some flashlights, though. I couldn't take anything from the house without my mom getting suspicious."

"I can get some and some extra batteries. Will we need sandwiches?"

"I don't think we're going to be gone that long. But maybe that's a good idea." The boys went to Henry's house to stock up.

A half-hour's ride brought them to the oldest part of town. They had never seen this section and stared in awe at the once glamorous mansions that were slowly decaying behind decorative iron fences. Perry kept an eye on the streets but didn't see the name, so they stopped to ask a passerby. Within a few minutes, they were standing in front of Grandmama's old house.

A three-story gabled light blue and white home faced them. It looked better than its neighbors, but they saw peeling paint and some skewed shutters, one hanging by a hinge. Perry pressed the front gate, which was four feet taller than they were, and it creaked open. Cautiously the boys entered. The lawn, once immaculate, was overgrown and weedy. Trees needed trimming. The front steps, concrete where they met the walk, were chipped in places. The wide veranda and wooden steps leading to it were in need of paint. Carefully, the boys made their way to the front door and found it locked.

"Now what?" Henry wanted to know.

"I read that these old houses could be entered through a basement window or cellar door. Let's see if we can get in that way."

They went back to the lawn and walked their bikes around the house. There were plenty of windows, but none that opened. The cellar door looked promising, but it was also a dead end. They stared at the house, feeling defeated.

"There's got to be a way in." Perry sounded determined. "Wait. We haven't tried the back door." They went there. It looked as if someone had forced it. Together, they pushed the door open. Perry closed it behind them and turned to find the basement steps right in front of them.

Flashlights on, they slowly descended into the basement. It appeared that Grandmama had not been down here in years. Layers of dust in varying thickness covered everything. Once kept orderly, it too was in disarray. Their jaws dropped at the sheer size of the basement. The house looked big from the outside, but now that they were inside, the space they needed to explore seemed positively huge.

Their feeling of defeat became overwhelming.

"What should we do?" Perry asked. "There's no way we can do this. There's just too much stuff!"

"Let's look only in boxes big enough to hold a big plate," Henry suggested. "I see a lot of small boxes here. If we ignore those, we can get through a lot of this today."

"Good idea. Let's start with these shelves." Perry indicated to his right. They picked a box off a lower shelf; moments later, they staggered back out into the sunlight, coughing and gasping for air. A large cloud of dust, something they hadn't considered, engulfed them when they moved the box.

The boys fumbled for water bottles and gulped the welcome liquid. Flopping on the overgrown lawn, they got their breath and decided on another plan. They would return tomorrow, tell their parents they were spending the day in the forest again, wear old clothes, get some gloves at the local hardware store, and tie some bandannas around their faces. Henry's mom would make sandwiches again, and they would take larger water bottles. Satisfied, after making sure the back door and front gate were secured, they pedaled to the forest for more frog finding.

The following day, the gardening gloves and bandannas helped a great deal as they investigated the basement. They found a lot of old clothes, family memorabilia, old newspapers and magazines, out-of-date canned goods, a well-stocked wine cellar, tools, some heavy silverware, old china dishes, furniture, pictures of a young man in an army uniform standing next to a World War I plane, but no silver plate. Discouraged again, the boys broke for a rest and a replan.

"This old house has an attic. What if we have to look up there, too?" Henry asked.

Perry groaned. "I couldn't do it today. I'm so dirty right now, it'll take - ugh! – *two* baths to get me clean again. I didn't think it would be this bad!"

"Me, either. I have to use the bathroom. Do you think there's one upstairs?"

"Yeah, has to be. Let's find out. We can at least wash our hands and faces." Perry looked at Henry and chuckled. Above the bandanna were two dark eyes and a dark face. He pulled his friend's bandanna off and chuckled. "You look like a raccoon,"

Henry returned the favor. "You, too. Let's clean up."

They went back upstairs, brushing and shaking the dust from their clothing on the way. Henry found the bathroom and was surprised at how spotless it was. Perry also was surprised. Given the condition of the basement, he never expected the first floor to be so clean and neat. While waiting for Henry, his eyes took in the large kitchen with its antique appliances and dining set, and he visually investigated as much of the dining room as possible without actually stepping into it. He looked behind to the back door, expecting to see black tracks left by his shoes. There were only light dusty ones.

Henry emerged, face dripping. "I didn't want to use the towel," he explained. "Everything is so clean!"

Now it was his turn to look around. Awed by the crystal chandelier in the dining room, Henry slowly edged into the room. A large antique table surrounded by twelve chairs commanded the center. To the right was a tall hutch filled with fine crystal stemware. Along the opposite wall was a buffet, topped by a large tureen and silver serving utensils. Henry quickly went to it and opened the double doors. Inside he found a great deal of fine China and some silver serving trays. A couple were too big to get into his saddlebag or even the sack he'd brought, but some smaller ones would fit just fine. He did not see any silver plate, however. He took a couple of small colorful plates and a medium-sized tray and put them into the sack. Perry stood by his side.

"Wow, look at all this. Grandmama must have done a lot of entertaining when she was younger."

"Looking at all these dishes reminds me that I'm very hungry. Let's get the sandwiches and water and then go home."

"Right. We can come back next week."

Once outside, Henry transferred the small plates, bandannas, and gloves to his saddlebags and fastened the sack firmly atop the bike's rear fender. They sat on the grass and ate lunch. Rested and energized, they walked their bikes to the front gate, once again making sure the back door was secure before leaving. They were ready to ride when a police car containing two of the town's finest pulled up in front of the house.

"Say boys," a policeman called from the passenger seat, "you haven't seen two burglars around here, have you?"

Henry and Perry gave each other surprised looks.

"No, sir, we haven't," Henry replied. "But if we had, we would have called you for sure."

The policeman unfolded his six-foot-plus frame from the vehicle and strolled over to them. "Well, that's nice to know, considering we think the burglars are you two." He looked at the sack to the bicycle. "Mind telling me what's in there?"

"It's a silver tray, sir." Henry was beginning to feel a little nervous.

"Uh-huh. And you found it where?"

"Perry and I came to his grandmother's house today to find a silver plate that she's always talking about. We didn't find a plate, but we did see this tray. So I took it to ask her if this is what she might have meant."

"Uh-huh," the policeman said again, pulling out a notebook and pen. "What are your names, boys?"

"Henry Smith Perry LaFarge." They spoke at the same time.

The policeman took the names. "You got a key for the house?"

"No, sir," Perry replied.

"Then how did you get in?"

The boys looked at each other. Both were feeling uncomfortable.

"We found the lock broken on the back door," Henry replied.

Perry was beginning to realize that they might be in some trouble, especially when he saw how dirty they were; the policeman would know that they were the ones who had gone through many boxes in the basement and had left the basement in worse shape than they had found it. They sure did look like burglars.

"Henry's telling the truth, sir. My grandmamma had an accident and came to live with us. She is always talking about a silver plate. I overheard my parents arguing about money. My mom wants Grandmama to live someplace where she can be taken care of, but there isn't enough money to put her there, so I thought if we found the plate she's always talking about, she could sell it and have money to live there. Then I could have my room back," he added.

"Ah. I see. And when did your grandmamma have this accident?"

"I'm not sure, but she came to stay with us about three weeks ago."

The policeman looked at the address on the house. " Don't go anywhere," he commanded and ambled back to the car to consult with his partner. After a few very uncomfortable minutes, he returned.

"What you're saying seems plausible, but I think we'll take you downtown anyway. Let's put your bikes in the trunk – *minus* the sack, please" – he indicated to Henry to untie it – "and check on your story further. In you go, boys." He ushered them into the back seat of the vehicle while his partner placed the bikes and the sack in the trunk.

Henry and Perry were totally taken aback. Both had visions of jail cells and nothing but bread and water for the rest of their lives. They were pretty miserable by the time they were seated next to the officer's desk at the police station.

They felt even worse when Mr. LaFarge stormed in forty-five minutes later to retrieve them. The officer explained to him they had received a call from a neighbor about burglars at the house, and Mr. LaFarge confirmed to the police what the boys had said about Grandmama; the officer said they wouldn't press charges and where to retrieve the sack and bicycles. No one said a word on the drive home. Mr. LaFarge dropped Henry off at his house and gave him his bike from the trunk. Henry thanked him miserably and slunk up to his house, where his mother waited in the doorway, arms folded and face stern. He and Perry waved a weak goodbye to each other. Henry wished he could be with Perry while his father reamed him out. He liked Mr. LaFarge, but the man was way stricter than his father, so he knew his friend was in for it. One look at his mother told him so was he.

Henry's father, summoned from work, was waiting in the living room. Glaring at his son, Mr. Smith intoned, "You'd better have a good explanation."

The boy felt as if he were facing his teacher with an incomplete assignment in his worst subject. Slowly, he began to explain the plan, why they concocted it, what they found at the house, and then the police came. Mr. LaFarge had taken the sack home with him, so he didn't have it anymore.

The Smiths heard their son out before saying anything. Then Mr. Smith said, "Why didn't Perry simply ask his parents for the key to the house? If you boys believed there was something valuable there that could help old Mrs. LaFarge, you should have said something."

Henry thought. "Perry never really said why, and I never thought to ask about a key. I just figured maybe there wasn't one. He told me he thought Grandmama was senile because she kept talking about this plate, and his dad said she'd never told him about it. Sometimes I think his parents don't really listen to him like you listen to me. I didn't tell you what we were going to do because I didn't think we were really doing anything wrong. We would go to the house, get the plate, and Perry would surprise his folks with it so they could sell it and get money to help Mrs. LaFarge. Well - " – Henry hung his head – "I guess I know better now. I'm sorry, Mom, Dad." He looked at them again. "I'm sorry. We didn't actually steal anything, did we?"

"You know that taking something without permission is stealing, Henry, but in this case, I don't think so." Mrs. Smith reached out a hand to her son. She looked at her husband. Henry just sat, miserable. She rose. "Stay here, son. Your father and I need to talk this over." A tear slid down Henry's face as he watched his parents leave the room. He wondered what was happening to Perry and if his friend were still alive.

At the moment, Perry was wishing mightily that he weren't. The LaFarges trusted their son completely, knowing that he usually made very good decisions, so this episode completely baffled them. Part of Mr. LaFarge's anger was in not understanding what had made Perry do something he considered completely stupid. He did not stop to consider his own eventful childhood nor the fact that his Grandmama never gave him a key to the house, nor did she ever mention one.

Like Henry, Perry was seated in the parlor facing his parents. Old Mrs. LaFarge was resting; Perry's father made sure the bedroom door was securely closed. "Talk!" was all he said, seating himself directly across from his son. Perry's mother sat in a chair off to the right; she was upset with Perry and also anxious for him, aware of what her husband's temper could unleash.

Perry talked. They listened. Mr. LaFarge also asked about the key and then realized his grandmother had never given him one. At least now, the boys' actions made some sense. Anton rose and motioned for his wife to follow him. They left Perry alone and miserable for what seemed to him the rest of the afternoon. Finally, his parents returned.

"Your mother and I have discussed the matter," Mr. LaFarge stated firmly, reseating himself. "This episode will not be mentioned to Grandmama. I will have the tray appraised, after which we will drive back to her house and replace it. I shall inquire about a key to the front door and have the back door repaired. You are confined to your room for the rest of the day and grounded for one week for lying to us about your actions. No television, no phone calls, no Henry. At the end of one week, full privileges will be restored if you promise never to lie to us again about what you are doing. During this week, you will contemplate what you have done and thank God that you and Henry do not have criminal records." His tone softened. "This world is not forgiving, son. Things could have turned out much differently for you and Henry if the policeman had not been understanding." He rose. "Dismissed."

"Yes, sir," Perry replied meekly, close to tears. He looked at his mother as he plodded toward his room. Her face held a mixture of concern and compassion, and her eyes gave her son hope that the end of the world had not arrived. Still, once in his room with the door closed, Perry flung himself onto the bed and allowed the dam to burst, misery and guilt swirling within. Crying himself to sleep didn't help; dreams of him and Henry in prison mixed with parental accusations and finger-pointing from his schoolmates swam through his brain. Grandmama's large sad eyes offered no comfort. Only his mother's soothing comments took away some of the stinging pain.

Henry, too, had been grounded, but only for three days. He moped around the house, trying to find interesting things to do, but nothing worked. He also had been asked to contemplate his actions and was glad the police didn't charge them with a crime. He tried, but failed to understand why grownups would do things so horrible to kids, especially to kindergarteners or first graders. He remembered at the age of five coming home from a shopping trip with a toy his parents didn't realize he had taken. They marched him right back to the store and had him return it, with a tearful apology, to the manager. The manager had been firm with him for stealing it, but in the end, seeing that Henry had not understood what he had done, gave him the toy, refusing his father's offer to pay for it. Henry had sworn never to touch another thing when shopping again, and he never had. From then on, he asked if he wanted something.

On the second afternoon of his grounding, Henry slouched into the kitchen and plopped down on a chair. "Mom, can I ask you a question?"

"Of course," Mrs. Smith replied, giving him a few potatoes to peel while he sat there.

"Why are grownups mean to kids?"

Startled, Mrs. Smith stopped what she was doing and faced her son. "Henry, where did that question come from!?"

"Well, I was thinking about what we did, and I remembered that store incident when I was five. The manager was upset with me, but he turned out to be nice about it. Why didn't he call the police?"

"Oh, he could have, I suppose," Mrs. Smith replied cautiously, searching her brain rapidly for answers. "I remember that, too. The toy only cost a couple of dollars, and we were willing to pay for it if necessary, but the manager used some common sense and saw the situation for what it was: a little boy not really understanding what it means to take something without paying for it. Maybe he remembered doing something similar when he was five." She touched Henry's shoulder, offering support and comfort. "People are so different today, Henry. This world has been going downhill for a long time. When my grandmother was a little girl, she could leave the house and not bother about locking the door. People respected authority then, and they don't do that so much now. There is so much more stress in the world today, and they have a hard time coping with it. That might be one reason. Another might be that they don't understand that children are not little grown-ups, and they need to be taught. If they do not teach their children the right things, the kids are going to get out of hand and do wrong things. Henry, this is a very hard question to answer! Some people are just bad and do bad things to others for who knows what reason. Others are misguided or ignorant. Some just can't cope with the responsibility of rearing a child. There are so many reasons that grownups mistreat kids. There isn't one single thing that you can say 'Aha! This is it.' Do you understand me?"

Henry peeled slowly, taking in his mother's words. "I think so."

"Oh, it's Perry, isn't it? You're worried about him."

"I am, Mom. I like the LaFarges, but Mr. LaFarge is super strict compared to you. I don't know what's happened to Perry."

"I see." She thought for a moment. "I'll talk to your father. Perhaps he can call Mr. LaFarge and talk to him. I know Anton is strict. Too strict, if you ask me." She went back to preparing her dinner, and Henry finished peeling the potatoes.

The next day, Henry climbed the big tree in the back yard to see if he could see his friend. All he saw was Grandmama sitting on the porch. The house seemed quiet. Perry apparently was not allowed outside. He leaned against the large branch for a while, and when it became obvious that his friend was not available, he climbed down and went back into the house. Henry was anxiously awaiting the following day because then he could go places again, but without Perry, it wouldn't be as much fun.

Two evenings following Perry's punishment, Anton LaFarge found himself dealing with very mixed feelings. On the one hand, he believed that once a punishment was put into place, it must be completed. On the other hand, he saw his son's suffering and wanted to modify or even stop it completely, restoring Perry's privileges. But then, was that not defeating the purpose of the punishment? He was being as strict with Perry as his father had been with him, but should he be? He had been very different when he was nine.

Perry's personality was quiet and studious, whereas he had been adventuresome and boisterous, skipping school if he felt the day was too glorious to spend indoors when the countryside offered so much to learn and explore. His insatiable curiosity made him an excellent biologist today, but back then, it had frequently gotten him into trouble. Anton still disliked his father's rigidness, but it eventually helped to channel his energy into a positive direction, giving him the drive to succeed splendidly at whatever he chose to accomplish. Perry was self-motivated, and all it took for him to spend hours at a task was to suggest that something wonderful lay beyond the obvious, and wouldn't it be grand to explore the concept to see where it led? Ergo the miniature wetlands in the basement. He looked at his son's pride in it and in his ability to maintain the ecosystem by himself, and saw that part of himself at nine years old in Perry. His son was a good boy, intelligent, and way more responsible about school and learning than he had been then, so what was the point in keeping him – well, imprisoned in his own house? Was that any different from being locked up in a cell? The criminal record, if you wanted to call it that, of truancy and troublemaking was his, Anton's, not Perry's. He did not want Perry to treat his children the way he had been treated. He perceived his father's rigidity and intolerance as tyrannical and hated him for it, and did not want to find himself in a similar position. He was sure his son loved and respected him, and suddenly it was important to him to maintain that love and respect. Perhaps, without realizing it, he was being his father, and the situation now did not call for it. All this was going through his mind when Adam Smith phoned.

They spoke for a long time. The next morning, Mr. LaFarge took Perry aside and asked his forgiveness for being the boy's grandfather instead of himself. He restored all of the privileges unconditionally, but was not too surprised when Perry did not immediately jump for joy and run to phone Henry that he was free. By the age of nine, Anton's skin had already developed some thickness; Perry's was still fragile. It would take a while for him to realize his dad was changing, and it would take time for Anton to feel comfortable with the change. Still, he noted, if they worked at it, the bond between them would one day be strong and secure.

Perry was totally surprised. He had learned very well when he was still small not to get his dad angry, and some of the punishments still twinged with mental pain. He did love Mr. LaFarge and was proud of his dad's accomplishments as a biologist, but he wanted and needed a dad, not a disciplinarian. He recognized that his father probably never would be like Henry's dad, but he didn't need him to be. All he wanted was not to be afraid that if he made a mistake like the one that just occurred, he would find someone with a nonjudgmental and understanding mind discussing it with him, not coming down on him like a sledgehammer. Perry forgave his father, but it took a full day's contemplation about him to adjust to and accept the changes that Mr. LaFarge earnestly wished to make. By that evening, he was his boyish self again. He phoned Henry to see what was happening to him, and would he be free the next day to see a movie or something?

Henry readily agreed and suggested a comedy, thinking that a lot of laughing would make them both feel better. It did, and by the following day, they were both back on the track of being boys enjoying summer vacation.

July and part of August came and went, and life was good. They began to pack as much fun and as many adventures as could be put into the days before school started again. Old Mrs. LaFarge continued to improve slowly and now walked with a walker. She and Perry developed a close relationship, the boy being fascinated by her life as a young woman, wife, mother, and then grandmother. She told him many stories of crossing the Atlantic to Europe on the great ocean liners and of the grand life she and her husband had lived in France and several places in America. Perry brought several different frogs and salamanders upstairs for her to see and marvel over and told her stories in return about their lives and where to find them, how they lived in the wild and in the basement, and Grandmama said when she was able to, she would go downstairs and see this marvelous creation for herself. She was a city girl, she said, and until she became too old to travel, her life revolved around big cities and charities and grand functions around the globe. To think that there was a microcosm of life living right beneath her was a revelation waiting to be revealed, and she was looking forward to seeing it. She spoke English most of the time now, and only once, about two weeks before school began, did she mention the silver plate again.

Perry wondered if he should tell her what he and Henry had done. His parents had not discussed her leaving since "The Incident," as they now called it, and her opening up to them had improved the relationship all around. He decided to ask Henry about it.

"Gosh, I don't know," Perry's friend replied when Perry brought up the subject. Then a thought hit him.

"What?" Perry asked.

"My saddlebags! I forgot all about them. I stashed them in the closet that night your dad took us home. The gloves and bandannas and – oh, goodness! – there are two small colorful plates in the bags! I totally forgot I put them there! We'd better give them to your dad."

They ran upstairs to Henry's room, and he dug the saddlebags out of the closet. Sure enough, under the dirty articles, were two shiny, colorful silver-backed plates a little larger than Mrs. Smith's dessert plates. The boys looked them over carefully and admired the workmanship of the filigree and colorful designs on the front. On the back was a funny mark they didn't understand.

"We'd better show these to my mom. She'll tell us what to do with them, so we don't get killed all over again," Henry said.

Mrs. Smith was surprised when she saw what they had. Henry explained that they weren't really sure what kind of silver plate to look for, as Mrs. LaFarge only spoke in general about a plate, but at the time, he thought that these might do. He'd forgotten about them as a result of the fallout from the parental explosion.

"Well, we'll have to return them to Mrs. LaFarge," Mrs. Smith said, admiring them also.

"What does that mark on the back mean?" Henry wanted to know.

Mrs. Smith turned a plate over and looked carefully at it. "This is the mark of the silversmith who made these. I don't recognize it, but I know someone who might. Would you boys be interested in a trip to the library?"

"Sure," they chorused, and fifteen minutes later, plates carefully wrapped in towels in a tote bag, they marched into the large public library that served their part of the city.

"Is Mr. DeLong in?" Mrs. Smith asked at the front desk.

"Should be. Take the escalator to the second floor, go down the hall to the right, and his office is three doors down on the left," was the reply.

A couple of minutes later, they stood before a door with a glass panel labeled, "Frank DeLong, Historian." Mrs. Smith knocked and opened the door. Mr. DeLong peered over his glasses and his highly cluttered desk as they entered.

"Well, upon my soul!" he exclaimed. "Maryanne Smith! Welcome, welcome!" He rose noisily, knocking a stack of papers to the floor and his chair against a bookshelf behind him as he came around the desk to greet them.

"Hello, Frank. Long time no see," Mrs. Smith smiled as they greeted each other warmly. "Frank, this is my son Henry and his friend Perry."

They all shook hands.

"What can I do for you, Maryanne? I take it this isn't just a personal visit."

"I have something to show you," Mrs. Smith said, taking a towel from the bag and handing it to Frank.

He unwrapped it and gave a low whistle.

"Where did you get this?"

"It belongs to a friend's grandmother. I thought you might be able to tell us something about it."

"Indeed, I can." Mr. Delong placed it carefully on the spot where the stack of papers had been and searched his bookshelf. "Ah! Here is what I want." He selected a large book and turned back to the desk, sitting unceremoniously back onto his chair. The visitors occupied whatever chairs they found, removing more stacks of papers.

"Ah, yes, this is what I'm looking for." Mr. Delong pored over a couple of pages of writing and figures for several moments. He turned the book and showed them a photo of a very similar plate.

"Here it is. You can read the history of it."

They crowded around the book and were amazed at the information given, including how it was first done by a Frenchman back in the mid-1500s. The history of the style, *plique-a-jour*, and its development into enameling on dinnerware by Russian artists fascinated them. Perry compared the plate he had to the picture given and was astonished at its similarity. Mr. Delong, meanwhile, referenced another book and showed the boys the current value of the plate he held.

All three were very excited when they left the library. Perry couldn't wait to tell his dad. Henry said since he had forgotten about them, he'd come along. Mrs. Smith suggested they wait at her house until they knew Mr. LaFarge would be home from work and then surprise him. Even she had a little trouble understanding that each plate was worth almost five thousand dollars!

The boys played catch to work off some of the excitement. Finally, six o'clock came. Perry called home to see if Dad had arrived yet, and was happy to hear he had. With a whoop, he replaced the receiver, leaving his mother to wonder what was happening.

"Dad! Dad!" Perry yelled, bursting into the house, Henry right behind with the tote bag. "I've got something to tell you! Really good news!"

The LaFarges were all at the kitchen table, anticipating indulging in the delicious food that accompanied the mouth-watering aromas from the oven. They were a little surprised to see Henry, too.

"What!" Mr. LaFarge extended an arm and gave Perry a hug. "What is such good news?"

Perry suddenly remembered the previous reaction from his father when he saw the silver tray and faltered.

He gave Henry a "Help me!" look, so Henry took a deep breath and jumped in.

"Hi, everybody. Ah – Mr. LaFarge, Perry told me about your – um – well, your concerns about Grandmama, so when we were at her house, in addition to the big tray, I also took two small plates. They were in my saddlebags on the bike, but I took the bags off and put them in my closet and forgot about them until today. Mom took us to meet a friend of hers at the library, and he showed us these plates in a book and looked to see how much they are worth." Henry pulled the towels out of the bag and placed them on the table in front of his friend's father. He unwrapped the towels to reveal the two *plique-a-jour* plates.

Grandmama's eyes grew big. "What!" she exclaimed, sitting suddenly upright. "How did you get these, and where did they come from?"

Perry's stomach did flip-flops, after which it tied itself into a tight knot. His heart started racing, and he thought his dad was going to have a cow when he saw his face. Mr. LaFarge felt like he was nine again, caught in a lie, having to face his father. Mrs. LaFarge just stared at the plates' beauty. But Grandmama called Henry over to her and again asked, "Where did you get these?"

"From the buffet in your house," Henry replied. He looked at Mr. Lafarge and at Perry, and then he got confused. "You mean you don't know?" he asked the elder Mrs. LaFarge.

"Know what? Anton, what have these boys been up to?"

Mr. LaFarge took a deep breath. "I can explain, Grandmama," he stated anxiously.

"*Non*! My great-grandson, he will explain!" her voice was commanding. "Come here, Pierre, and tell me what you did. Does it have something to do with your being – how you say – being put in the ground?"

Perry slunk over to his great-grandmother. She did not appear to be angry, but he wasn't certain how she felt. He gave his dad an uncertain look as she put a frail arm around him. Mr. LaFarge nodded slightly, his face betraying his nervousness.

"I was grounded, Grandmama, because I wanted to help you, but everything went very wrong!" Tears welled up, and he fought them back. Grandmama reached for a napkin and gave it to her grandson.

"There, there, it can't be all that bad, can it?" She looked at him curiously, face tilted slightly, and gave him a gentle squeeze. Perry felt better but still found it difficult to talk.

"I – overheard my parents arguing one night about your stay here. They weren't sure what would happen to you, and they didn't know if there was enough money for you, so I decided to go to your house to find the silver plate you were always talking about when you came here. I thought maybe Dad could sell it and give you the money to live on. So Henry and I went to your house to find the plate. We couldn't get in at first, but we found the back door open, so we went in. Everything was so dusty in the basement that we had to come back the next day with gloves and bandanas for our faces, and we looked in boxes to find your plate. We didn't find anything, so we washed up upstairs before leaving. Henry looked in the buffet in your dining room and found a big tray and these plates. When we left, the police took us to the station, and Dad had to come and get us. I was grounded because I lied about where we were going. All I wanted to do was surprise you and give you some money to live on, Grandmama! I didn't mean to do anything wrong!" He started to sniffle in spite of himself.

"It was my fault, Mrs. LaFarge." Henry was now standing next to her and Perry. "I put the small plates in the saddlebags on my bike and forgot about them until today. My mom took us to the library, and a friend of hers looked up the plates in a book. They're worth a lot of money, ma'am, five thousand apiece. Mom's friend told us where you could sell them if you need the money."

The LaFarges gasped at the plates' value. Old Mrs. LaFarge looked from one boy to the other and then at the parents as her mind processed the information. Everybody seemed to be staring at her as if it were her move.

"Well!" she exclaimed, as if that settled everything. "Let me get this straight. You, Anton, thought I was a burden to you, even though you took me in out of kindness, yes?"

Alice and Anton both protested at once. Mrs. LaFarge listened for a moment, then held up her hand.

"Stop!" she commanded. They both became instantly silent. She eyed Perry and then Henry.

"You, Pierre, thought you would help your poor Grandmama by finding a plate I kept talking about and give it to me to sell so I could have money. And you, Henry, being the good friend, went with him to help him find it. Where is the tray, Anton?"

"It's in a sack in the closet. I had it appraised, and it's also worth about five thousand. I have not yet gotten back to your house to replace it and fix the rear door, Grandmama."

"Good. Now. Pierre, do not cry. You did nothing wrong. You were helping me from the kindness of your heart. You are a good boy. You gave up your beautiful room for me and you went to my house to find the plate that would bring me out of poverty. Remember that I said I would not forget your kindness for giving up your room?"

"Yes, Grandmama," Perry sniffled.

"I have not forgotten, nor shall I." She was thoughtful for several minutes. No one said a word. Then she said, "I have decided." She looked at each in turn.

"Anton! You will sell the tray at Rochester's Auction for the five thousand dollars. Put that money into a bank account toward Pierre's college education. Alice! You have never once indicated to me that you were uncomfortable with my stay here. Always, you were gracious and kind. However, since I am much better now, I have decided to go back to my house to live. No, no!" She raised her hand at the protests that burst from everyone's lips. "I have decided. The boys were able to get in the back door because the paramedics had to break in to get me when I fell in the kitchen. I kept the doors always locked, which I am not going to do again. Pierre! Because you at such a young age have such compassion and caring for such an old lady as me, I am giving you one of these plates." She chuckled at his astonished reaction. "Keep it. When you have your own children, you will teach them to be like you and show them this plate as a reminder that love begets love." She gave him a squeeze. " And Henri." She pronounced it the French way, which to him sounded like "Hone-ry." "I had completely forgotten these plates existed. It has been what? Twenty years since I entertained? I will sell the second plate and give you – how much do you want? Five hundred? A thousand, eh? You tell me."

Henry was totally surprised.

"I don't really want anything, Mrs. LaFarge. I just was helping Perry, that's all."

"Then, I will decide what to give you, and you will take it, yes?"

"Um – yes, I guess so." Henry was still taken aback at the unexpected offer.

"I have a whole set of this dinnerware, which I will have auctioned off. Those thousands of dollars should keep me for the rest of my life. I am 102, and how much longer can I live? I shall hire a full-time housekeeper and fix my house and yard. That should help the property values, and perhaps some of those old wrecks will sell, and the area will look good again, no? And Pierre, I shall give your good friend a thousand dollars for his education and maybe – " she winked at Henry – "a new bike when you outgrow the one you have." She stopped momentarily. "But tell me, Pierre – this plate you were looking for. You said that *I* spoke about it all the time? I do not remember such a thing, and I don't think, given the look on your parents' faces, that they remember it, either."

"Yes, Grandmama." The boy had recovered. "When you first came here, you spoke French more than English, and you kept saying something to my parents about a silver plate. You usually ended your sentences with the words."

Mrs. LaFarge's eyebrows furrowed. "*Non, mon cher*, I do not remember –" she broke off as a thought struck her; her eyes widened, and then she began to laugh, a high, cackling laugh that to Perry had not been used for a long, long time. "Oh," she gasped between cackles, "I know now what you mean. You are a smart boy, *mon* Pierre. If you hadn't heard what you heard, you would never have gone to my house and found these wonderful old dishes that now have given me a new look on my life, as you all have. It has been wonderful being here, but now I must make the plans to move back home." She gave Perry as hard a squeeze as she could and then pulled his face down to hers for a kiss.

"Shame on you, Anton, for not believing your son. I did indeed speak of a silver plate but in *French*. Pierre heard me in *English*. That misunderstanding gave me my independence again. Thank you." Perry received another kiss.

"Misunderstanding, Grandmama?" Mr. Lafarge asked, baffled.

"But of course! What sounds like 'silver plate,' Anton? Surely you could have figured it out!"

Mr. Lafarge thought a moment, and then he too began laughing, as did Alice. The boys just looked blank.

"Pierre," Grandmama said with a smile and a twinkle in her eye, "It is time we all had something to eat, including you, Henri. Take the wonderful supper from the oven and place it on the table, *if – you – please*. Perhaps I should say it the way you understand, Pierre – 'sil – ver plate,' or, more <u>properly</u> – "she paused for effect - "*s'il vous plait*."

After the Door Shuts

After the door shuts and the footsteps die, I lie listening for the next sound. I'm alone in the room. Not that I want to be, you understand; it's just the way it is. I'm the outcast now, you see, needing the soft darkness and the quiet nights. Youth and health brought plenty of friends and family flocking around, but life hands out lemons sometimes, and I didn't know how to make lemonade. So when my health and age went south, well, it seems everyone else did, too.

Oh, they try. Sometimes someone will toss me the proverbial bone to perk me up, but I've lost interest. They will occasionally take me somewhere to get me out, but I usually end up staying in the car while they go and have their fun, do the errands, whatever. They think I don't understand what they mean when they speak of the "poor old guy," but hey, inflection speaks louder than words. They treat me condescendingly and think I don't know it. Come on, I wasn't born yesterday, although to me, it seems like it.

Ah, well. I can't move like I want to. The hips hurt. My heart has problems, and of course, I'm overweight. Too much rich food I shouldn't have eaten. Some members of the family smoked, so the secondhand smoke got at my lungs. I wheeze and cough. It scares the younger members of the family, but not me. One thing I can say for myself, I was tough. I worked hard and played hard. Now-hmph.

There. There is the sound I was waiting for, the footsteps I have been longing to hear for months. The door opens, and he stands there, outlined by the bright lights beyond. His arms reach out for His old friend, and a soft "come" is the most welcome word I've heard in ages. Without thinking, I leap out of my bed into the grasp of a big hug.

"Time to go," His gentle voice says. I glance back at my sprawling, lifeless body, and bark happily. The road back to Heaven is short, and my Creator has many toys waiting for me.

The Eye of the Beholder

Collapsing under a canopy of green leaves, the elf king lay as quietly as he could while gasping for breath. What had started out as a quiet morning stroll turned into a nightmare chase under tree trunks, through flowers, vines, and mushrooms, and over a rock pile. Odini had never before seen such a monster whose mouth had moments before missed him by a fraction of an inch. Only a sharp turn into a mouse hole had saved him. The monster rushed by and kept on going. The mouse had chosen a place for his burrow well: the entrance was covered by a thick group of large leaves that, viewed from the outside, didn't appear to be anything other than a bunch of leaves at the base of a tree. The only reason Odini knew it was there was because a fellow elf had shown it to him only the previous week. The mouse was a friend of the other elf, Raki, and Raki had encountered this monster himself two weeks before.

Odini continued to lie there. His breathing was better now, but he did not wish to move yet. His keen ears could hear the beast snuffling about near the entrance. Then from a distance, he heard a noise that sounded like a call, and the snuffling became a roar and then stopped. His ears rang from the loudness of the sound, and he winced and involuntarily put his hands over them. When he took his hands away, Odini became aware of another sound: almost silent breathing from about two feet away.

Carefully, slowly, he turned his head in that direction and beheld a large brown mouse sitting on its haunches, looking quizzically at him.

Odini took in a large breath and spoke evenly and quietly.

"I am Odini, the elf king. To whom may I have the pleasure of speaking?"

"Sit up, man, I'm not going to hurt you. I can see you're an elf. I'm Aoki, the mouse king in these parts. Don't get your knickers in a knot over that thing that chased you. I have it on good authority that it won't hurt you if it doesn't like your taste. Moth told me." Aoki extended a paw. "Come on, man, you need some nourishment after that chase." He came over to Odini and gently helped him up.

They stood for a moment, looking at each other over. Aoki saw a tall, thin elf whose brightly colored blouse and tights were torn and stained with dirt. Odini saw a tall, somewhat dumpy mouse whose eyes were friendly and whose manner was a bit raffish. Aoki led him through a convoluted burrow into a slightly disheveled room well lit by a couple of candle ends. He motioned the elf to sit on a stone while he busied himself with getting herbs and brewing tea. It smelled good, and Odini realized he was hungry as well as thirsty.

"Raki showed me your burrow entrance last week. Thank God he did, or I might not be here right now."

"Good elf, that Raki," Aoki replied. He pulled a couple of tiny plates from a slightly skewed cabinet and set them on a mushroom cap near Odini's seat. These were followed by two odd colored cups now steaming with brew. The mouse then placed a couple of sunflower seeds on each plate.

"Drink, man, the tea won't stay hot forever." Aoki took a seed in both paws and began to nibble. Odini followed suit.

"What do you know about this beast?" the elf asked between bites.

"This," Aoki replied, spitting a couple of pieces of seed as he spoke. "It's new to the neighborhood. Only been here about a month or so. Doesn't come by every day, if you know what I mean." He swallowed and took some tea. "Couple of my subjects have had close calls, and one actually was caught and shaken by the thing. Shook so hard, he flew out of its mouth and got knocked out by hitting a tree. Good thing, too. The beast just sniffed him and walked away. I saw it from a distance, so when the thing was out of sight, I ran over and helped my fellow mouse get up and get medical treatment. Got a whole line of herbs in my storeroom. When you're a mouse, you gotta know herbal medicine or man, you can be a goner in seconds." Aoki finished his seeds and tea and replaced them with more. "Here." He stuck a plateful of seeds under Odini's face. "Elf yourself." He chuckled at his pun.

"Thank you." The elf took another seed and began to eat it. "I really didn't get that good a look at it, being rather occupied with getting away, but what I saw seemed more frightening than being chased by it. It seems to have a lot of long teeth that mean business and is covered by curly silver spikes."

"That it does." Aoki poured them more tea. "It has long legs good for running and hot breath that can fry your fur. Funny thing, though." Aoki paused and frowned. "According to my subjects, the breath doesn't smell. Most beasts have breath that would stop a clock, if not a train. So I don't know what to make of that."

The dishes on the mushroom began to vibrate, then rattle. Aoki's ears and whiskers stood at attention. His eyes widened as he assessed the increasing shaking. "Come on," he cried, motioning for Odini to follow. Running quickly back to the entrance of his hole, elf at his heels, Aoki stopped suddenly, holding his paw to keep Odini back. Very carefully, they crept forward; Aoki parted two leaves just enough for them to peer out.

Attached by a chain, the beast was trotting unconcerned beside two giants, who were the cause of the shaking ground. Aoki noticed the giants' feet were covered by large shoes with wavy thick rubber soles. Their huge bodies sported a shiny material that glistened as sunbeams broke through the trees. Flora crunched under their feet as they passed. They were roaring at each other, but the mouse spoke a spell that quieted the noise and then said another that translated the roaring into a speech he and Odini could understand.

"...drive was amazing," one was saying to the other. "I am so glad we came here for the holiday. Little Booboo has been having a ball, chasing mice and other small creatures. Oh, now what? No, no, Booboo, come on." The speaking giant stopped, bent over, and lifted the beast, whose nose had gotten uncomfortably close to Aoki and Odini. The beast received a hug. "You're a good little Yorkie, aren't you? Speaking of which, on our way back to the States, I'd like to visit Yorkshire to see if...." Their voices faded as the two Americans continued walking on their Sherwood Forest tour.

Night Train to Chicago

Nobody noticed me as I shuffled along the walkway to the Pullman car, ticket for a family sleeping room in my inside jacket pocket. If anyone did notice, they pretended not to. Why should they? A somewhat stooped old man, messed-up hair in need of a wash, out-of-date clothes that had definitely seen better days, old loafers that needed polishing...that I had a huge portfolio that brought in enough for me to live well on off the interest, plus several sizeable CDs, was nobody's business but mine. I had fifty dollars in small bills in my right pants pocket, but nobody could see that; the trousers were a bit baggy, enough to hide the small wad of bills. Passengers rushed past me to and from the depot. Trains hissed, horns blew, and announcements blared, causing some to cover their ears. My hearing is no longer good, so I didn't care.

I found my car and climbed aboard. Getting up the narrow curved stairs proved to be a bit of a challenge; my knees needed replacements, but I was not interested. They don't hurt too badly on humid days, and on dry ones, they weren't even noticeable. Fortunately, Los Angeles humidity isn't that high, and I no longer live next to the ocean.

A couple of young, strong men strode past me, causing me to bump into the wall. They didn't even mumble "Sorry" as they went past. For all I knew, they never saw me. That was fine with me.

My room was on the far end in a corner. The bright light inside felt welcoming. The room consisted of two beds, two seats facing each other, and a private bathroom. Community toilets don't work out well when you have heart pills, water pills, arthritis, and you don't walk fast.

I had to get away from this city. It was almost time for the nightmares to start, and it was becoming too difficult to bear them any longer. Months of therapy had not helped, and I felt that they would continue until my death, which will be close. By the time the train pulls into the Chicago station, two-and-a-half days from now, two of them will have tormented me. I wake up screaming now. Hopefully, the noise of the train will drown out some of the screams. Probably not.

My beat-up Rolex sounded the half-hour. Seven-thirty on a Friday night. Sunday will see me at Lake Michigan, where I plan to board a ferry to its namesake state. The crossing takes only 2 – ½ hours. They're usually crowded. No one will notice an old man slip over the side in the middle of the lake. I hope the day is sunny. I like sunny days.

Don't worry. My lawyer will receive a letter in the mail on Monday. It will tell him of my suicide and give instructions on how to dispose of my estate. The money goes to various charities and legal agencies and to a private family in the poorer section of Los Angeles. I hope it helps. It won't bring back their son, but it will give them the ability to buy a house in a nicer neighborhood and start fresh. Old memories in old surroundings never bring healing. I know. I've lived with mine long enough.

The conductor walks through, calling the imminent departure. I feel anxious. It's been years since I've ridden a train. In fact, I can't even remember the last time. Fifty years ago, maybe? Something like that. If I needed to go anywhere, I either flew or drove. This should be an interesting experience.

I remember riding trains to visit relatives a hundred miles away when I was a kid. The diesels were fast and powerful, and the little boy that I was loved it. The rides were smooth and quiet, and I look forward to a similar trip.

The car jerks as the train starts. It jerks again one or two more times, then settles into the rhythm of the wheels. The Pullman door is open, as is my door, and I can hear the "clackety-clack" as the wheels ride over the tracks. I like the sound; it's soothing.

A short time later, the conductor comes by for my ticket. I hand it to him. He looks it over and then at me. His eyes search my person for recognition. "Yes, it's me," I tell him. "I need the privacy and the space. I do hope a family wasn't displaced by my choice of accommodation."

"Not likely, sir," the conductor replies respectfully. "The dining car is two cars back and opens at six tomorrow morning. Breakfast will start at six and go until nine. Lunch is from twelve to two-thirty, and dinner is served from five until seven-thirty. My name is Edward, sir, and any questions or problems, you can call on me. The porter will help you with your luggage when we get to Chicago."

"I don't have any," I reply softly. "My trip is one way, as you see, and whatever I need in Chicago, I can purchase there. My length of stay there is uncertain at this time."

"Very good, sir. There is a call bell for emergencies right to the side of the door here" – he pointed it out – "so if there is a problem, please don't hesitate to use it."

"Thank you, Edward," I reply. He touched his cap, closed my door, and I was alone.

I turned the bright light off so I could look out the window without seeing reflections of everything in the room. The window in the door provided enough light and a small reflection in the glass. Pressing my nose against the glass caused it to fog from my breath. Can't win for losing. Shifting in the seat helped block the hallway light, and now I can see out.

Hm. Not much to see. So many tracks, so many trains. We're not going fast yet. It will be a while before we clear this area. Freight trains are waiting to get to the places where they will be unloaded. We pass a waiting passenger train. Sleepy people look back at us. They can't see me in the dark. I don't want to be seen.

The conductor recognized me. Such is the price of fame. I don't think he'll tell anyone. This is not the me I used to be. Sometimes I would like to be that person again, but it's better this way. Guess I shouldn't have given my real name when purchasing the ticket. It no longer matters, actually. In sixty hours or less, my life will be over. My lawyer might miss me, but no one else will. Having never married has its pluses and minuses. Right now, it's a major plus.

The train is finally reaching the outskirts of the city. According to the map, it will turn north once we're through the mountains, going through Victorville and Barstow. It will stop at Needles to take on and discharge passengers, and then continue on to Flagstaff, where it will stop again. By the time it reaches New Mexico, it will be daylight. That's good. I like to look at the desert and buttes.

The rocking rhythm is soothing. Sleep forces my eyes shut. I fight it. No luck. It's daylight when I wake. The train isn't moving. That's good. I'm stiff and need to use the restroom. Should have brought my cane. It would help when the train is moving, even slowly.

After washing up, I sit again. My stomach growls, letting me know it needs food. Should I ignore it or not? I look out the window. People mill about the platform. An Indian woman approaches some people with a tray of handmade jewelry. She sells a few pieces and moves on. A faraway horn blasts twice. The people begin to board the train. Soon we are moving again.

Hunger gnaws. When was my last meal? Yesterday at what? Noon? Good grief. No wonder I feel a little rocky.

Right now, the ride is slow and smooth. I risk going to the dining car. I travel along the top level and am forced to descend the narrow, small steps at the end of the car. The coach is noisy. It's a blessing to reach my destination. The line isn't long, and I am soon seated at a table. The waiter sizes me up and figures I'm good for nothing. He most likely thinks I can't pay for the juice, coffee, bacon, eggs, and toast. He is surprised when he gets a decent tip.

As I leave the table, my peripheral vision catches sight of an elderly gentleman in a sky blue silk shirt. He is seated on the opposite side of the aisle, two tables up. I turn to look, and he gives me a small smile and goes back to buttering his toast. I continue back to my room.

Once seated, an image of the gentleman pops into my head. He has a full head of wavy white hair and a white beard to match. The image nags me about something that doesn't come through. I put him out of my mind and let the rocking motion of the car put me back to sleep.

I wake up somewhere in New Mexico. A butte sits in the distance, and I wonder what it would be like to see the world from the top of it. If I had a bucket list, that would be on it, but I don't. The seat is comfortable, and my mind goes blank except for taking in the scenery. The day is sunny, and it looks warm out there. The sleeper is cool, perhaps too much so, but it's not bothering me particularly. The train begins up a slope. It slows to take a curve. The diesel engine becomes visible. Too bad they switched. Sixty years ago, one could still travel by steam locomotive. They were magnificent and powerful, a siren for dreams of a young boy. Now dreams are nightmares.

Nightmares. Tonight they begin. No matter how much I try to find ways to relieve myself of them, they come. The young man, his fainting mother, the decision that ruined my life....

....It was an ordinary day on the bench. I sat through the usual cases: wife beater, drug dealer, a divorcee wanting more money and custody of the child she'd never get back because her mind was no longer functional, petty larceny. Stuff that had become a bit run-of-the-mill. Still, I wouldn't have changed it for anything. My hard work and studying made me a top lawyer, then put me in the courtroom as a judge. I pored over cases, sometimes not getting to bed until the wee hours, then spent the day hearing the case that kept me up all night. Gradually my reputation as a fair judge grew. Lawyers on both sides liked being in my courtroom. There was no nonsense. For those cases not involving a jury, the time spent hearing and arguing was usually quick. Experience is a good teacher, and she'd taught me well. I knew what to look for, what to listen for, and how it was presented. Even some of the criminals who came before me, at least the better class, thanked me for hearing their case. I firmly believed in the law, in honesty, and in fairness in giving sentences. Few cases over a twenty-year period were ever challenged.

Then came the toughest case I'd ever heard. A young man, who had just turned eighteen when he came before me in a jury trial, had been accused of robbery at a convenience store during which the owner was shot and a customer was killed. His name was common enough – Jose Garcia. How many of those lived in my city of two million people, I wondered. I'd reviewed the case the night before, so I had a fair idea of what to expect. It was the unexpected that ruined me.

It started out the usual way – young kid, poor family, no money, sick parent. Unfortunate circumstances, to be sure, but there are other ways of getting money without robbing a store. The young man sat quietly with his lawyer, head down; the prosecutor was sparing no horses in his fervent delivery. The injured owner, arm in a sling, sat at a table behind him. The family of the deceased customer sat on the opposite side of the court, faces grim or teary. The mother of Jose sat directly behind him, her face a mask. Never having had time for a wife and family, I could only guess at what she might be hiding behind the façade. We were soon to find out.

The lawyer for the defendant came up. He called witnesses, refuted everything the prosecutor said, and presented new evidence that would confirm the boy's innocence. I called a recess for thirty minutes and took the lawyers into my chambers. They argued and played their roles well. Not much was settled by the time we came back. I admitted the new evidence into the trial. The defendant's counsel explained it to the jury.

I called the young man to the witness chair. He sat on the edge, having sworn on a Bible to tell the truth. He looked at his mother, and my eyes followed his. She was staring at him, fear and love in her eyes, and I could almost feel her prayers. She appeared to be pale. I wondered if she would faint.

The boy vehemently denied every accusation, stating that he was innocent, and they had the wrong person. I watched him. His own fear, and also some anger, was very real. He said the police forced him into confessing, that he was nowhere near the store when the alleged incident took place, that he was several miles away at his girlfriend's place saying goodbye to her before that family left for a South American vacation. Could he prove it? He said he could, but that no one listened to him. The family was not available to speak with, and his other friends were doing their own thing that day, so only the people on the bus saw him. I asked him if any of the witnesses who testified were on the bus that day, and he said yes, that the driver and the lady he sat next to were in court. I asked him if he could get in touch with his girlfriend; he stated they went to a village in the Andes where there was no phone service. Despite the two witnesses, who did not do too well under cross-examination, the cards seemed stacked against this boy. I reminded the jury that they had to consider all the evidence fairly and not be swayed by rhetoric or sympathy. They went out to deliberate. I called a recess.

The young man rushed to his mother, holding her against him. I told the bailiff to keep an eye on her in case she fainted. I went back to my chambers for a soda and a sandwich.

The jury returned in two hours. Everyone sat silently as they waited for the verdict to be read. The young man and his mother clung to each other; one of her hands was very busy with a rosary. The lead juror stood.

"Have you reached a verdict?" I asked.

"We have, Your Honor."

"Please read your verdict."

"We find that Jose Garcia is guilty of robbery with intent to kill."

Mrs. Garcia screamed and did faint. Jose tried in vain to revive her. The bailiff went to them, calling for assistance on his radio. The rest of the room was in an uproar, the prosecutor smiling, the defense lawyer trying to talk to his client, and everyone else either congratulating or complaining. It took some minutes to restore order.

I called Jose to the bench. His face was white, his black eyes round with fear.

"I am INNOCENT!" he screamed at me. I raised my hands for silence and looked at him closely. There was innocence in his eyes. I saw it with my own and knew it in my heart. It tore me up to have to pronounce a punishment for him.

A thought broke in. *"You don't have to punish this boy, Judge. You saw his innocence. You know it for yourself to be true. You can sentence him and then reverse it, stating your own views. He should not go to jail."*

I was torn. I knew I knew that he was innocent. It was in his eyes and heart. Could I agree with the jury or send them back for another round, telling them to search their hearts as well as their minds for facts that would exonerate him? As a judge, I had the final word.

It was also my duty to uphold the law. A jury of – well, they weren't exactly his peers, as many of them were at least ten years older, if not twenty. They had done their civic duty.

Another thought came in that I was an elected judge sworn to uphold the law, and if a jury found the defendant guilty, sentence must be declared. If further information was found that indicated an incorrect verdict, a new trial could be held. Perhaps the defense lawyer could get more information that could throw new light on the case.

I called him forward. He was thoroughly disgusted with the verdict, seeing as I did that the boy was innocent, a victim of circumstantial evidence. The bailiff reminded me that I needed to pronounce a sentence. The lawyer asked that I do so, but stay the sentence until further evidence could be found. Was there any?

With heavy heart, I gave the young man the lightest sentence possible under the circumstances and ordered him sent to a minimum-security prison. He just looked at me, his face registering no emotion. I wished he would have screamed, ranted, hollered, something! Jose just stood there until the bailiff led him away.

I felt like a total heel.

Indeed, the case nagged me incessantly until a week-and-a-half later, I asked for his file. It was brought to my chambers the next day. I rescheduled all my cases for the next two days and mentally barricaded myself in my rooms. I took that file apart paper by paper. Nothing. Noticing it was six p.m. and I hadn't eaten since breakfast, I boxed the file and took it home with me. After a light supper, I went to my den and started all over again.

Another three hours produced nothing. There was evidence for his innocence, but the prosecutor had done his homework well, and the evidence for his guilt overrode it. I searched intently through each document, looking for a sentence, a word, anything that would cause me to reverse my judgment. Zero. Zip. Nada.

Disgusted to the nth degree, I put everything back into the file and slammed it down on the right side of my desk. A small piece of paper floated out to the floor. I almost missed it. This one I hadn't seen before. It must have been stuck inside the folder. I read it. I read it again. And again. *This was what I was searching for!* It was just a note scribbled onto a piece of paper, but that note would clear the boy.

"Dumb Spanish kid," it read. "Forced confession too easy. Need to make it harder next time." There were two initials: J.D.

I thought it over and decided J.D. must work for the Homicide department.

First thing the next morning, I called Homicide and spoke with the lieutenant in charge. He gave me three names with initials J.D.: John Davidson, Joseph Darling, and James Davenport. I asked him to fax over any public information on the three men. Half an hour later, it arrived.

Davidson was the one that had some questionable items on his record. He was known to dislike Latinos, had successfully defended himself in a lawsuit charging racial profiling, and was strict about enforcing curfew and other laws in his district. Now I needed a sample of his handwriting to compare it. There had been sworn statements by the police in the file. I reopened it and searched for his statements. Yes, there they were. A comparison of the first initials of the name confirmed my thought – they were the same.

I drove at once to the courthouse. I was able to get the verdict annulled. I was also able to get Jose Garcia released from prison that same day. Between phone calls and faxes, by noon, the jail had the order to release him immediately.

It came too late.

At 11:30 a.m. Jose Garcia had been murdered by an enraged inmate in a dispute over nothing.

The absolute injustice of the whole situation hit me hard. I had only myself to blame for the loss of that life. I really didn't HAVE to have sentenced him. I could have taken different routes, made different choices pending acquisition of new information. Now I had to offer my sympathy to a devastated family

There was nothing I could say to them that could or would give them comfort. Forever I would be the man who sentenced the boy to death. There were family members who saw it that way. His mother refused to see me. It would be months before she phoned to say that she had forgiven me, followed a second later by a dead line.

The cop who framed the boy got fifteen years. For all I cared, it could have been fifteen minutes. From that time on, my life went slowly and steadily downhill.

Time heals, it is said. Not so for me or Jose. I'd read the report of the incident that took his life. During free time, some lowlife, a quiet man who cycled through the prison periodically and never gave any trouble, had without warning accused the boy of taking his comb. Jose denied it, and the man went berserk, slamming the boy against a wall and beating his face with hammerlike fists and the strength of Superman. It took four guards to separate them. An ambulance was called, but the paramedics pronounced Jose dead. The coroner's office did an autopsy. The blunt force caused veins within the brain to rupture, and the boy's neck was broken just under the brain stem. Reading that made me very sick. I felt like murdering the man who did it. The boy did not need to die like that; he did not need to die at all.

But he did.

The murderer was sent to a maximum-security prison for life. Psychiatrists stated that a buildup of a common depressant in his system caused him to hallucinate and experience feelings of paranoia; he thought that inmates were constantly taking his belongings, and Jose's denial of any theft put him over the edge. He was kept under strict supervision, and his medication changed, but it was too late for him, too. Had he understood what he'd done, he probably would have wished he'd made any decision but the one he did.

He died there five years later.

As for me, I voluntarily resigned from the bench a year after Jose's passing. Life had become hell for me, watching others who looked at me and wondering if they knew what I'd done and if they judged me as harshly as I was judging myself. They must be. An upright judge who could send an innocent young man to prison, even a minimum-security prison, was not worthy of his job.

Jose's face began to appear in my dreams. At first, it was just fleeting, here and there, once every long while. As the years went on, it happened more frequently, and the visits were longer. Once, he sat on my former seat and looked at me, looking up at him, being judged by him. That one woke me in a cold sweat.

I felt chained. Almost everyone had tried to support me in one way or another, telling me it was just very unfortunate timing that had freed the boy permanently, that in fact, I'd done a very noble thing by getting the order to free him in less than three hours when normally the process could have taken much more time. I'd never told anyone, even God, about my internal indecision that day of the sentencing. Gradually, it ate away at my feelings of self-worth. Over a period of years, even as I'd slowly been able to push the memories into my subconscious, I became more and more depressed and down on myself. Even after having become a staunch advocate for freeing innocent prisoners, my life took on a meaning of futility. Nothing could erase what I'd done, and nothing would ever cause me to think of myself as worthy of anything again.

I lived on the income from my savings and investments and the sale of my big house; a little one in a nice neighborhood that was on the edge of turning seedy if the economy took a big enough downturn (it did and, as the saying goes, there went the neighborhood) was good enough for me. Eventually, my clothes became Modern St. Vincent de Paul instead of Macy's. I didn't care. It was what I deserved.

The nightmares began several months ago. Jose sat on the bench and accused me of murder. Huge police officers dragged me away and put me in a cell with heavy iron bars. I pleaded to be released, but no one heard, my voice echoing into nothingness. The dreams gradually got more intense until one evening, I thought I saw Jose standing in my bedroom, watching me as I prepared for bed. He never said anything. Just stood there and looked young and innocent. It was in the dreams that his head began to –

A jolt broke my reverie. I suddenly realized where I was. Sunlight poured through the window as the train made its way north from still another small-town station. I checked my watch. Six p.m. Had my memories been so strong that I'd missed lunch?

A knock on my door startled me. It was Edward, who wanted to know if I'd be going to the dining car. He'd seen my progress, or lack of it, that morning and offered to help me walk. The train began rocking a bit as it picked up speed, and I said yes, that would be nice. Having someone to hold on to was a blessing.

This time I was seated at a table across from the bearded man. He smiled at me, and again, a nagging feeling, this time of vague recognition, filled me. I wondered if he'd been one of the individuals I'd judged or if he'd been a professional of sorts working behind the scenes in the courthouse, being seen here and there as he went about his job. I smiled back slightly and gave him a nod.

"Nice day today," he said conversationally. "Did you happen to see the forest we snaked through? It was magnificent."

"Um, no," I replied. "I, uhh, fell asleep for a while today." The lie wasn't totally white. I had felt myself nodding off while recalling the events that brought me to this moment.

"Pity," he said. "Perhaps on the return trip, you'll see it."

"I have a one-way ticket." I quickly glanced at a menu a waiter gave me and ordered. He left.

The man looked at me as if he found my statement very interesting. "One way, is it? How far are you going?"

"Chicago."

"Ah." He buttered a roll. "We will be pulling into Kansas City tomorrow morning. I'm attending a conference there." The waiter came and poured his coffee and offered a basket of more rolls. The man shook his head. I took them instead.

"These are excellent rolls. You really should try them. They are very light, and have a buttery flavor that is enhanced by adding more butter, believe it or not."

I didn't feel like eating really, but had to. So I tried one. He was correct.

"The train will lay over a couple of hours in Kansas City. It's a good place to stretch your legs. There are many interesting sites near the depot, and the depot itself has a unique architecture." He looked me over. "We appear to be about the same age. Did you like trains when you were a boy?"

For some reason, that question launched me into happy memories of riding and dreaming about them. The man listened with interest. His food arrived, and I interrupted my narrative long enough to tell him to eat it. He did, but kept one eye and ear tuned to me. Even when my food arrived shortly thereafter, I kept talking. He urged me to eat, so I did. The silence during that time was welcome.

More and more, I felt like I knew him from somewhere. Well, I'd seen thousands of people during my life in court, so it must have been from there. Probably a staff worker from many years ago.

My reticence to open myself to another slowly dissipated.

After supper, he asked me where my room was. I told him, and he offered to walk me there.

"I saw you come in with Edward," he said. Those stairs are awkward to climb, I know. It's no trouble at all for me to help you back to your room. I have a room one car over, so you must be in the one after mine."

"Yes," I acknowledged.

"Good. Shall we?" He offered an arm.

Surprisingly, the walk back was easy. The train hardly rocked, even though it was moving at a fairly good rate. The man made sure I was seated comfortably before leaving.

"By the way," he said thoughtfully, "I find you a very knowlegeable companion. Would you mind meeting for breakfast at seven-thirty tomorrow? I really would like to continue conversing with you."

I found myself agreeing, though not knowing why. He was friendly, quietly open, and just emanated good vibrations. For some reason, I felt no resistance to the offer.

"Good night, then." He left, closing the door after him and giving a small wave through the glass as he started back to his own room.

It never occurred to me that I didn't even know his name.

At 7:25 the next morning, just as I was getting ready to leave, a light knock caused me to turn. It was my new friend, for that is how I now thought of him. I opened the door and greeted him.

"It is a good morning," he replied with a grin. Extending an arm, he again asked, "Shall we?"

"We shall, indeed," I answered. I stepped outside the door and closed it. The train was rocking a bit now, so he took my arm and carefully guided me along the hallway to the steps.

"I will go first," he said, "and help you down. Grab the railing with your right hand and give me your left."

He proceeded down three steps and turned, right hand extended. I bent slightly and grabbed it. He had a strong, reassuring grip. Between the railing and his assistance, I made it down safely, even though the train seemed to go over a bump of some sort and jolted slightly. For some reason, his presence made me feel more secure and safe.

There was no problem being seated. We got a nice view for a change. Shade trees and grass, prairie in the distance, and sunny skies made for a promising day. That thought surprised me. Looking forward to a day, me? It's been a long time – wait. There was no nightmare last night, either! That surprised me even more.

"Penny for your thoughts," my friend almost whispered.

"Nightmares! There wasn't a nightmare last night." My voice had a wondering quality to it, not to mention almost happy.

"How wonderful!" Then, as an afterthought, "Do you get them often?"

"Quite often, for months now. I wake up screaming."

He looked very concerned. "I'm so sorry. Did you sleep well, then?"

I couldn't remember, actually. "Must have."

He smiled.

"Well, then, I'd say you're going to have a good day. Let's order now. Then we can talk."

By being careful, my money would last through tomorrow. There were always ATMs if it didn't, but my card was at home in the dresser drawer. Didn't matter. There were enough banks around.

The waiter brought coffees and glasses of water with a little ice in them. He left with two orders of the same breakfast. Funny how this fellow's mind worked like mine.

"We'll be in Kansas City in a couple of hours. Perhaps you'd like to use the layover time to get out and stretch. There will be plenty of time for you to get back to your room."

"Yeah. Yeah, that sounds like a good idea." Actually, I hadn't even thought about it until he mentioned it. But why not? Even though my ambulation wasn't that fast, one foot still went before the other. Too much sitting made me stiff, and my body felt it. "Where would we go? I can't walk too far."

"I know this town well. There's a park not too far from the station. We can go there if you like. Walking through a green, grassy park is always an uplifting thing."

It didn't really matter, so I agreed. All the while, I'd been studying my friend's face. Somehow, I knew him. He looked at me curiously.

"Oh, I do apologize. I didn't mean to stare at you, but more and more, I think I know you."

"Oh, I'm sure you do. Think back to your childhood. We were friends then."

Being studious, I'd never had a lot of friends, and the ones I did have went in different directions after grade and high school. I figured he must have been a grade school pal, but I still couldn't quite place him.

After some thought, I gave up.

"I'm not sure. How did you recognize me after all these years? After all, I don't look anything like a kid anymore."

"Let's just say I'd know you anywhere. Do you remember George Watson?"

George Watson…it took a while, but finally, a memory slipped in. George Watson. The freckled kid with a shock of light hair that never understood what "comb" meant. The smartest kid in the school, who had a sense of humor that would have made Charlie Chaplin proud, the kindest boy anyone had ever met, but who would not hesitate to put a bully in his place, verbally or physically. We were thick as thieves then. I stared at my friend again. There was some resemblance.

"George? Is that you, really?! Looks like you've done well!"

"I'd say you've done well, Roland."

Roland. No one had called me that in years, and I mean years. I was always known as Chris, short for Christopher, my middle name. After I became a lawyer, it was R.C. Cauldwell. Then Judge Cauldwell. I thought about that. Hah. Some judge I turned out to be. One of the less savory names I'd been called over the years seems to fit me a lot better now.

The waiter brought breakfast. We ate in semi-silence, each thinking our own thoughts. George and I went our separate ways after the second year of high school when his family moved to Missouri. We wrote sporadically, and after a card for my high school graduation, I didn't hear from him again.

After the waiter took our plates, I got up to leave. George walked me back to my room again. I went to the bathroom, and when I came out, he was seated across from my usual place. That was interesting. Was this going to be Old Home Week? I wasn't sure how much I wanted to talk to him.

"I think we need to talk, Roland," he said gently, yet there was a sound in his voice that brooked no refusal. So I sat. He gently took me through my childhood, and the great times we had. We even formed our own "church," he playing God and me playing the sinner. Even as children, we explored our lives and our relationship with the Trinity through this play. Not until we parted did I realize how much I'd come to know the Trinity. We had to read the Bible, of course, to act out many of the incidents in both the Old and the New Testaments. Our understanding was that of children, and then the line, "Let the little children come unto Me," popped into my brain.

I asked him about it. George grinned.

"Actually, that's a favorite line of mine," he said, "especially after my son became a teacher. He taught everyone, but his favorites were small children. He related well to them."

"I never had any children – or a wife. It's been just me all my life. Sometimes I wonder what life would have been like had I taken that route. It just never occurred to me to do it, not really."

"Believe it or not, I followed your career with interest, especially after you became the district judge. You did very well on the bench."

"Yeah." I looked at the floor. There was a long, heavy silence between us. Then George said kindly, "Do you want to talk about it? Is something wrong? Please tell me."

I didn't look up. "George, we're too old to be playing 'church.'"

"Considering that my life has been one big ministry, I disagree."

"You're a clergyman? For real?!" My head jerked up to face him.

"I suppose you could call me that. My ministry is helping others. I let my son do the teaching."

This information floored me. My brain fumbled around, trying to think of something to say. Edward knocked on the door and opened it.

"Kansas City depot in twenty minutes," he announced.

George looked at his watch. "My goodness, this time flew by." He stood. "I will be back, Roland, to help you detrain. A walk around the park and some good old Midwest sunshine will do you a world of good." He smiled, and somehow I knew he was right.

Nodding, I told him I'd see him in a few. It was with some reluctance that I prepared to leave the train.

Then I remembered the pills I'd forgotten to take earlier. The day's supply went into my shirt pocket.

Surely the depot would have water fountains.

Visions of Chicago floated through my brain. The determination and plan of suicide didn't seem so strong now. What had changed? Was that really the only way to go? I was alone in many ways, so what did it matter? The world wouldn't miss another bum, which role my somewhat wrinkled clothes certainly confirmed.

George was beside me. He took my arm, I looked one more time at the room, and then we started down the hallway. There was a line in front of us. Everyone else must have had the same idea about disembarking. The train rocked gently as it slowed for a stop. Rock…rock…JOLT! The cars seemed to bounce off one another as the train came to a halt. George almost lost his balance; a wall held me up.

"I'll have to have a word with that engineer," he mumbled.

"You know him?" This friend contained a lot of surprises.

"Yes. I helped put him through school. He loves traveling, so after a couple of false starts, he gave up the regular business world and learned to be a railroad engineer. He's done pretty well for himself, but life must be a bit off now, or he never would have stopped the train like that. I've ridden his route several times, and he's always been careful and conscientious about his engines and passengers. Something is bothering him a lot if he's driving like this."

It was our turn to go down the steps. George helped me as before, and within minutes we were halfway to the depot.

Kansas City. It had a lot to say for itself. Popularized in the musical "Oklahoma!", an old West cattle town, home of a great university, and, I soon discovered, it had a busy, modern, lovely downtown. George went to check on his luggage. I found a water fountain and downed the pills.

Soon he was back. "I sent my luggage to the hotel. I'm a regular there, and there's one particular bellman who will take care of it. Let's go on to the park. The weather is excellent today."

We crossed a busy street and went a couple of blocks down. It was amazing how the landscape changed. From hustle and bustle to quiet and bucolic in two blocks flat. I stared at the lushness of the lawn and the greenness of the trees, bushes, and plants. I think Chicago has a park like this, too. Maybe I'd see it if time permitted.

We sat on a bench, enjoying the light warm breeze and bright sunshine. It made me squint. George handed me his sunglasses. Under protest, he got me to put them on. They fit fine, and my eyes didn't tear up from the brightness.

"Let's walk this way. There's a botanical garden over here I think you'd like."

Like it? I loved it! Such an array of color and beauty I'd never seen. Flowers, blooming bushes, plants of every variety imaginable hit my brain as if it had been dropped into a hundred colors of paint. I marveled at the sight. We slowly walked around, taking everything in. Even the busy nearby basketball courts and distant tennis courts radiated fun and serenity. Such peace. I hadn't felt this way in years.

George's gentle prodding finally got me to open up about Jose Garcia, as much as it pained me to do so. I hadn't intended to tell anyone about it, but once the words started, a floodgate opened. We continued to walk as I told him about the decision, the feelings, the unfortunate timing of Jose's death, the family's response, and my downhill slide. He said nothing until I'd finished. I was about to ask him what he thought when something punched me hard in the chest. It took my breath away, and I fell backward.

I must have been unconscious for a few moments because George was doing chest compressions on me when I came to. I waved his hands away and attempted to sit up. That didn't work, and I found myself on my back again. He let me lie among the flowers for a few minutes until my breath came evenly, then extended a hand. I took it. He helped me sit up.

"Shall I call an ambulance?"

I sensed my body. It seemed all right now. There was no pain. I took a couple of deep breaths. Everything seemed fine. My pulse was steady. I looked around for a basketball but saw none. It must have been picked up by whoever ran after it.

"Let me just sit for a minute," I told him. "What hit me?"

"Hit you? I don't know. One moment you were walking beside me, the next you were on the ground as if something had knocked you down. How do you feel?"

"Actually, better than I've felt since I don't know when. Well, yes, I do. Since Jose Garcia's travesty of a trial."

"Roland, you must not think like that. It was the decision you made among all the choices– I read the papers – but you did what you thought you had to do at that moment. Other people have gone through what you have done. Some have beaten themselves up as you did, others didn't. Guilt is not pleasant to deal with, but judging yourself the way you did brought you to this point. Do you really think suicide is the answer for you?"

I felt well enough to move. "Help me up. It must be time to get back to the train."

George stepped in front of me and extended his hand.

"Don't worry. I'm quite strong. Ready? One…two…three aaaaand…UP!"

A moment later, I was back on my feet. I thought I'd feel shaky or wobbly but actually felt good. George repositioned himself at my side, threw an arm around me as he'd done when we were teens, and we started off again. We walked back through the flowers and down a side path into a wide expanse of a lovely park. We spoke as we did years ago, and I began to feel much better. He certainly knew how to minister to someone. I was glad we were together.

My mind must have wandered, because suddenly I heard him say, "…and you never learned to forgive yourself. You judged yourself much more harshly than God ever would have and allowed yourself to sink into a morass of guilt and judgment. By talking to me, you finally rid yourself of all that darkness and heaviness. Guilt can punish you more than the law of the universe would, you should know that."

We were on a wider path now, one that inclined slightly. The park now looked like a piece of prairie, with brown and green grasses intermingling. In the distance, I could see part of what looked like a city behind a lot of trees, and I guessed we were heading back to the depot by a roundabout way, one which I would not have wanted to miss.

"Forgive yourself, Roland." George's voice cut through my thoughts. "Please, look into yourself and see yourself for the great guy you are. Let God be your judge when you finally face him. He has all the information about that situation. He knows a lot more about it than you do. Oh, here comes someone I want you to meet."

From the large group of trees, about a quarter-mile away, a young man emerged. George continued to support me and urged me again to forgive myself.

"Look, you told me about the burden you've carried for so many years. By doing so, you have opened yourself up to God's forgiveness. Let Him forgive you! Then you have to forgive yourself. Can you do that?"

"You're not playing God again, are you?" I laughed.

George chuckled. "No, I am not playing God again. But I need to hear you say you forgive yourself. There is no sense in carrying that kind of burden. Can you do that?"

I looked at myself, in scuffed up shoes and old wrinkled clothes, a bum who soon would be fish food. It was a hard decision to make, but eventually, since I felt much better about myself, forgiveness seemed now to be possible. So I took the leap.

"Yes, George, I forgive myself."

"Do you mean it? For real?"

I had to laugh. "Yes, I mean it. FOR REAL!"

Suddenly, I felt great. It seemed like my minister friend had erased years of a dark burden that now appeared so unbelievably heavy that I wondered how in the world I'd carried it. My body even felt as if it were floating.

The young man walked rapidly and momentarily would be close enough to speak to.

"George, I don't know how you did that, but your minister training certainly has done well by you. I don't know how to thank you. I mean – I feel so wonderful, even better than before I tried young Garcia's case."

"Roland, you did a heck of a job researching that file. That cop needed to go down. He'd been wringing false confessions out of young people for years. Some of them never got out of prison and died there. His hatred for people he'd never even met was so unjust. The prison they sent him to had a good chaplain. That cop really needed to hear about God."

George turned to the young man, who had stopped to join us.

"Roland, I want you to meet someone. Actually, I think you know him. Jose Garcia."

I just about jumped out of my skin, the shock was so great. Jose looked even younger than when he was before me in court, not at all like the downtrodden, miserable spirit that had haunted me for years and caused my nightmares. He smiled at me. George took my right arm and held it out to Jose. We shook hands.

"Judge Cauldwell, I forgave you years ago, and so did my mother. She will be very happy to get the money. She needs to move out of that house, and now she can. My family and I thank you for your generosity."

I couldn't even say anything. George and Jose just laughed.

"George, are you playing some kind of joke on me?" Anger was bubbling up. From a wonderful high to crash to earth with this horrible joke was too much.

"No, Roland, I'm not playing a joke on you. Turn around."

He took my shoulders and gently maneuvered me so I could see the park and the place where I'd fallen. Something dark lay there. It seemed so far away and yet so near, as if I were looking down at it from a great distance, but not so far that I couldn't recognize what looked like a person lying among the flowers. It took me a moment to recognize my own body. George's grip on my shoulders was steadying and comforting and firm.

I looked at him, then turned to look at Jose. He was smiling, his eyes innocent and pure. He was here, but couldn't be. George was here, or was he? Where was I?

"Judge Cauldwell, I was directed here to welcome you to your new home."

"What new home? I'm on my way to Chicago to take a ferry to Michigan and quietly fall overboard. I'm committing suicide." Why Jose had to hear that was a mystery to me.

"No, Judge, no. You are here with me and George." He broke into a laugh, as did George.

"Roland, my friend, *you* see George here before you. I loved the way the two of you played Me when you were children. You asked Me if I was playing God, and I said no, which is the truth. You see, I AM God, and I came to bring you home! The lake is a cold, unforgiving place to die. That is why you needed to unburden yourself and forgive yourself; I'd already done so. You should have listened to your colleagues when they told you it was unfortunate timing that Jose was murdered just before he could have gotten out. You couldn't know that he pulled that murder in order that your soul could be saved. You were on the path of self-righteousness and didn't know it. You would not have gone to a good place today had we not intervened."

"*Si*, Judge Cauldwell. This was all planned out before I was born. I agreed to get murdered so that bad cop could be brought to his own justice and so that you could be brought back to heaven where you can be with the REAL George Watson, who came here a couple of Earth years ago. You didn't need to go through all that darkness, but because you did, you can better appreciate the light that you will now experience."

Somehow, everything made sense. The anger was gone, and I was in the light of God and a beautiful young spirit who was willing to die a horrible death – to save ... ME???

"As 'George' told you earlier, you're a great guy, and you made a great judge. That one lousy decision you made actually put you on the path to salvation. And here you are!"

It was real, and it wasn't. I hadn't planned on dying today. I wanted to go on my terms. But life doesn't always give you what you want. I would have died on the train. When alive, expect the unexpected. God's plan was so much better than mine. I wasted years of my life in guilt. Such foolishness, I know now.

The former George Watson and I had a great reunion. Our playing "church" had had a reality to it. It taught me about God's love and forgiveness, something I'd forgotten when self-righteousness crept in.

How ironic. George playing God gave me the spiritual knowledge that I'd built my life on, and God playing George brought me back to it when my guilt derailed Him.

I look at my surroundings and at the lake where I'd planned to die. It did seem very cold and dark. The park was such a beautiful place to leave the earth, and I'm glad my death happened there. I'm happy I made the decisions on the train that I did. I hadn't known before about our being able to plan our lives with Him before we are born on the Earth. So many times, once we're here, we stray from the path we were meant to take. Sometimes it's our decisions, sometimes our parents don't listen to what we have in our child hearts, and our path deviates. Either way, we have to trust Him that He's guiding us. Never would I have planned my death in a beautiful park. But I'm glad He did.

When you deal with life - and God - you never know what to expect. You feel like dirt, and He hands you the flowers that grow in it. All I could do was shake my head and grin at Jose. I flung my arm around his shoulders and we walked back along the path to the city in the distance.

And the city wasn't the train's layover point, either.

King Lun's Challenge

King Lun, a beautiful Maine Coon tricolor cat, lived in a lovely palace, surrounded by all kinds of gardens and fish ponds. He had wise advisers and was loved by his citizens. His kingdom was peaceful and calm. The days went by in orderly fashion, as did the seasons. The sun rose and set, and the moon waxed and waned. Seldom did anything disturb the peace of mind of the citizens of the kingdom.

Far away across the mountains was another kingdom, but it was not peaceful. Bad things didn't happen, but events often caused for alarm or dissention. The cats there were reasonably happy, but often one could hear them wish for a little boredom. Life was – well, not hectic, but full of events, strange or exciting or unusual. King Popo, also a Maine Coon, had his hands full to keep his kingdom on an even keel.

One evening, just as the King had finished a rushed meal after a hectic day, a guard came hurrying in with unusual news.

"Oh, Your Majesty, please come to the courtyard at once! A farmer is there with a most unusual animal!"

That piqued the King's interest.

"An unusual animal, you say? How so?? Does it look strange? Is it polka-dotted? Does it have more than the standard number of eyes, ears, feet??"

"It looks perfectly normal to me, your Highness, but the farmer claims it can jump higher than any other animal in the world!"

"Really! This I have to see!" At once the King leaped to his feet and rushed out to the courtyard to see this marvelous creature.

He wasn't sure what to expect, but what he saw wasn't it. He flung open the palace doors and ran into the courtyard to find –

A cow.

The big, luminous eyes gazed at him peacefully while the gyrating mouth munched on a bunch of flowers the King had just planted that day. The farmer stood a couple of feet away, his left hand holding a rope attached to the cow's neck and his right respectfully holding his cap. He bowed low as the King arrived.

"Holy Mackerel!" King Popo exclaimed, eyes wide.

"If it pleases your Holiness," the peasant replied, still bowed, "this is a cow."

"Yes, yes, I can see that!" King Popo snapped. "But besides eating my prize flowers, what else can it do!?"

"It jumps, Your Regalness."

The King was calmer now. "It jumps," he repeated.

"Yes, Your Royal One," the farmer replied. "How many cows do you know can do that?"

"Well –" The king looked doubtful. "None. I do not know any cows that can jump. You say it can jump higher than any animal in the world?"

"Yes, O Doubtful One. I hope tonight to show you what it can do."

"I had planned on spending a quiet evening with my wife. On the other hand, knowing my wife, the evening will not be very quiet. So I look forward to seeing your cow jump. Does it have a name?"

"Her name is Astrid, my lord."

Astrid backed up a couple of steps and helped herself to another bunch of flowers. The King grew upset.

"Take Astrid away from my flower beds!" he cried. "Let her stand in the middle of the courtyard away from anything edible!"

The farmer calmly tugged the rope. The cow, munching away, just looked at him.

"Astrid, you must do your best for the King tonight! Do not eat his flowers! Where are your manners!"

Astrid swallowed the flowers and mooed softly. Then, of her own accord, she moved to the center of the courtyard and stood still. Her head went up and she mooed again, louder this time. Everyone looked to see what she was staring at.

The sun had set behind the palace, and the sky was baby to deep blue, filled with pink and orange puffball clouds. Peeking out from behind one of them was the moon.

The cow gave a long, low moo, as if longing to be with the moon. King Popo looked at the farmer.

"What's with her?" he asked.

"She loves being in the moonlight, O Noble One. She does not come into the barn like the other cows do. She stays outside and gazes at the moon. She has been known to run around the pasture, leap over the fence, and follow the moon's path as it sets. I think she would live there, if she could."

"Be that as it may," King Popo said, "I want to see her jump." He turned to his guard, who had followed him out. "Call my grand wizard! I want to know what the highest jump any animal has made is, including us!"

"At once, Your Lowliness!" The guard turned and ran back into the palace.

Astrid was becoming restless. She looked at the enclosed area and decided it wasn't for her. Without even mooing "excuse me," she began walking around the palace to the other side. The farmer tried to hold her back but ended up running after her when the cow broke into a gallop.

King Popo puffed after them. "She's strong and fast!" he gasped.

"She is, your Excellence. That is why she is such a great jumper! You will see very soon!"

Behind the palace was a very long walkway, cutting through the center of the gardens. It was at the beginning of this walkway that Astrid stopped. She looked at the moon, which now was almost overhead and clear of clouds, and turned her head to look at the farmer, who nodded.

Astrid went rigid. Then she relaxed and began to move down the walkway. She broke into a run, then a gallop, then an all-out gallop, and –

"OMG!" King Popo cried. His eyes bugged out as he watched the cow launch herself into the air and go up, up, up until she was a mere speck in the sky. Her shadow moved over the face of the moon as she cleared it by a hundred feet. The King rubbed his eyes, not believing what he saw. Astrid's speck gradually increased in size as she came back to earth. Everyone, including the Grand Wizard, saw her come down. But where she landed, they couldn't say. Everyone rushed to the back wall of the gardens, but it was too high to see over. The guard gave the King a leg up and peered over the wall. No cow.

"Where is she?" shouted the King to the farmer.

"Probably landed a few miles down the road. She'll come back here, O Astounded One. Be here in a couple of hours or so. Then we can talk about business."

"Business?"

"Surely, you would want such a magnificent animal for your own, Your Excellence. No one else in the world can do what Astrid does."

The King thought for a while. "You're right," he told the farmer. "If I had such an animal, I'd be world-famous! Think of the tourists she'd bring in! Goodness knows, the money would help pay for all the damages caused by all the unusual events around here. How much?"

"She is yours for free, O Frugal One, if there is no one else who can top her feat. My suggestion, O Creative One, is to hold a contest. If anyone can jump as high or higher than Astrid, I will work as your personal servant for the rest of one of our lives. If not – my village is very poor, Your Indulgent One, and a few hundred thousand would not be amiss."

The King figured he'd just gotten himself another servant, so he said, "Deal!" They shook paws to seal it. Then he sent the Grand Wizard for drinks and desserts, his question forgotten.

Sure enough, about three hours later, Astrid strolled in. She looked smug and proud of herself. The King greeted her and led her to his flower beds. He figured she deserved it.

Word of the cow's feat spread quickly. Astrid repeated the feat the next night with all of the town watching. Cheers reached the cow's ears as she descended gracefully onto the far border of the next county. Three hours later, she was back at the village, with garlands of flowers being draped around her neck and a bucket of the finest water from the best spring available placed before her. The King and the Farmer were very proud of her. The King congratulated him, the cow and, silently, himself.

Within a week, word of the feat reached the delicate, silky ears of King Lun. He sat astonished as his advisors told him of the effortless bovine leaps. Then he became consternated.

"A cow! A cow! Impossible." He began to pace as thoughts flew around his head. He could not let this go unchallenged! Why, his ancestors were the very finest and fittest cats in the world, held by the highest esteem of all rulers. No, no. This could not do! A bulky piece of dog meat leap over the moon, his beautiful, luminous moon with its pastel light gently and tenderly kissing the night? No, this would not do.

He, a sleek, graceful Maine Coon revered of the kings and princes of generations past, a relative of lions, cheetahs, and jaguars, would rise to challenge!

He called for his wisest advisor, How Fat, and asked him, "How high did this cow actually jump?"

"She cleared the moon by a hundred feet, I was told."

"A hundred feet." King Lun thought. Then he asked, "I believe I heard that King Popo's contest is open for one year?"

"That is correct, Your Majesty."

"How Fat, I want you to collect all of my astrologers, all of my advisors, and my former gym instructor and discover what signs prevail for the coming year, the percent of the possibility of my defeating this cow, and what the latest gym wear is. I shall defeat this animal and win silly King Popo's contest. Oh, and I also want to know when the best day will be to attempt this feat."

"Yes, Your majesty. When would you like your answer?"

"Preferably, as soon as possible."

How Fat bowed. "On my way, my King."

"Oh, and include the dietician as well. If there is a food I should not eat, I will drop it. If there is one I should include, I will add it. I will beat this silly chunk of dog meat by a mile, if necessary."

How Fat bowed again and left. King Lun went outside to the swing in his garden and sat, moving gently back and forth as his mind went in various sized circles around the challenge.

Two days later, King Lun had his answers.

He found out that the signs and omens for the coming year were very favorable and predicted a high chance of winning. The most favorable day to challenge was the second last day of the challenge year, the hottest gym wear was "Pink Silk", and adding two extra fish and seven cups of green tea with protein per week would improve his health and strength by 37% if he would also add cardio and squats to his workout.

"Done!" exclaimed the King. "I begin at once! Tell my gym instructor to purchase new workout clothes for me, and I shall meet him in the garden in an hour!"

How Fat bowed and left to find Lu Tein.

King Lun went to his chambers, disrobed, and entered the little meditation room next to the royal baths. He prayed himself into a trance and lay sphinx-like, until three minutes before he was to meet with the instructor. Dismissing the visions and voices from his mind, the King rose, stretched full out, and left the room. He strolled to the windows overlooking the garden, peered out, and smiled. Waiting below was Lu Tein, clothing draped over a front leg and new shoes beside his worn ones. King Lun leaped from his window to the tree and climbed nimbly down to meet with his friend and teacher.

How Fat watched from a distance. He'd always admired the King's physical prowess, and watching him now did not diminish that admiration. He thought King Lun did not need a year's workout to beat a cow, but then, he hadn't seen the cow in action. He decided he might just stroll over to the next kingdom for a look.

Against medical advice and common sense, King Lun wore himself out the first day of his new regimen. The moon shone on an empty swing that night. A week later, after assiduously caring for very sore muscles, the

King was ready to proceed at the recommended pace. This worked, and week by week, his strength and agility improved. A month later, he was able to leap into his favorite tree from a distance of ten feet. If he stood at the foot of the tree and leaped, he could land on some of the low branches, and the swaying of the branches improved his balance. By the end of two months, he could clear the tree.

Six months later, as he sat on his swing and crooned softly to the moon, he wondered what it would be like to land there. He would have his advisors look up moon landings and see what they were like.

He was astonished to discover humans used rocket ships to fly to the moon and that it took a couple of days to get there. Humans, being so much larger than cats, should have been able to jump there without any help whatsoever. That was before he learned that the moon was 221,500 miles from the earth at its closest point, that he would have to leave the earth's atmosphere and gravitational pull to get there, and calculate mathematically the amount of thrust necessary for him to accomplish this feat, given the temperature and general climatic conditions. He could not comprehend attaching his seven-pound self to a rocket requiring several thousand pounds of fuel and then taking several days to arrive at his beloved moon, not to mention float or fly or whatever it was that spaces shuttles did to maneuver over it.

He had one night to do the same.

King Lun had trained seriously and steadily and was nowhere near his former sleek kingly self. He now resembled a muscular cheetah, whose speed and distance he could equal without even getting winded.

Now he began to train furiously.

His subjects wondered what was taking place daily behind palace walls. They knew something was up, but not what. Rumors began spreading, as well as general dishevelment as the town's and countryside's usual government maintenance began to slide. Trees became overgrown and leafy, garbage collection became spotty, street maintenance went from every week to every two or less, and the King's semi-weekly appearances dropped to zero. Finally, a local official complained to the palace.

When How Fat discovered what was going on, he went to locate the King immediately. He found King Lun hanging upside down by a toe atop a large lilac bush.

"Your Majesty, I must see you at once!" How Fat exclaimed.

Startled, King Lun fell to the ground, twisting to land on his feet.

"How Fat! How DARE you interrupt me!" the cat snarled.

The advisor was completely taken aback, but he managed to recover quickly.

"Your Majesty, the townsfolk are complaining, and rightfully so." How Fat quickly outlined the problems.

"I will get to them in two hours when I finish my workout!" King Lun snapped. "Now go! Collect the advisors and have them meet me in the meeting room then. Not a moment before will I see them! I have much to do!"

With that, King Lun, forgetting he fell from a bush and not a tree, leaped fifteen feet into the air and, with an unholy yowl, splashed into the koi pond on the other side.

Two hours later, a group of highly concerned and offended advisors verbally pounced on the King as he came through the doors of the meeting room and told him not only where things were at, but also how, which, why, when, what kind of, and how many.

They also told him off.

Chastened, the King hung his head and very humbly apologized. He had not realized that in attempting to beat Astrid's jump, he had made himself unavailable to everyone except Lu Tein. Training had taken over his life, and the kingdom suffered because of it. He immediately issued orders to set everything right.

Three days later, everything was back to normal, and the subjects loved him again.

After that, King Lun worked out in the morning, met with his advisors and the town or country officials for three hours after lunch, and then worked out again until early evening. Sometimes after that, he would swing on his swing and croon for a while at his beloved moon. Sometimes he would sing himself to sleep and wake up next morning curled up on the ground. Then he would yawn, stretch, and start his workout again.

One more month went by. Then Lu Tein said, "It is time to work out in the mountains, Majesty. You have mastered the easy stuff. Now it's time to put your skills to the test. Everything you have accomplished here can be applied there. Today you rest. Tomorrow we leave for the Butterscotch Mountains, and get that gleam out of your eye. They will provide sticky situations, but not sweet ones. There are three mountains. You must master the tallest one by one week before your jump. You will then rest for four days, meditate for two, and eat only protein the day we go to King Popo's country. You will rest peacefully that night and meditate again the next day. That night, you will complete your jump. How Fat stated that Astrid cleared the moon by 100 feet. You must jump higher than that, even if it's only an inch. Then you will have proven that cats are superior to cows and everyone else because no one else can do what you did. Are we clear on that?"

"Yes, Lu Tein, very," King Lun calmly replied.

"Good. We will take ten changes of clothing each. Those rocks are unforgiving, and clothes will be torn. Four of your palanquin bearers are available, yes?"

"Well, yes, but won't I be walking there with you?"

"No, Majesty. You will be carried and meditate for the whole time. I will walk beside you and meditate also. Our combined mental energies should produce some very powerful visions."

"The ancestors will be watching, yes?" King Lun inquired.

"They will probably be making bets among themselves over how high you will jump, Majesty. So, yes, they will definitely be watching."

"Good. I must not forget to light candles at the graves tonight."

"A good idea, Your Highness. Give my regards to Shining Moon."

"My moon will be – oh, yes, of course, *that* Shining Moon. I love my moon very much and for a moment –" the King broke off. "I will choose my clothing carefully. Whoever sees us must know that their King is passing."

"Majesty, one robe will do. The ten changes refer to your gym clothes. They will easily fit inside your palanquin. We should make steady progress and be in the foothills within the week. The weather gods smile upon you. The journey will be pleasant."

"Good. I bid you farewell, then, Lu Tein. We shall meet here tomorrow morning at –?"

"Sunrise, Your Majesty. Sleep well." Lu Tein bowed and left.

King Lun crossed the east garden and entered the cemetery where several generations of his ancestors, kings and queens all, slept away their eternity. He lit candles at each gravesite, saying a small prayer for each. At the gate, he bowed solemnly to them, stepped outside and closed the gate gently, then walked slowly back to the place, memories peacefully invading his thoughts.

Shining Moon's spirit rose from where she slept. She yawned and stretched long and luxuriously. One by one, other ancestors awakened and joined her. She was extremely fond of her grandson, but this evening her thoughts were not quite grandmotherly.

"I say, old girl," Shining Moon's husband, Flying Tiger, said, floating up beside her, "the grandson's gone a bit bonkers, eh what?"

"I thought you dropped that British accent half a century ago," Shining Moon replied, smiling. "Oh, yes, I forgot – it comes back when you're upset. Yes, I believe he has. Imagine – falling for that old nursery rhyme scam. Jump over the moon, indeed!"

"Agreed," Lotus Blossom, King Lun's mother, stated, joining them. "But I will admit, all the exercise is working wonders on his body and mind. I've never seen him so fit, even when as a teenager, he worked out like crazy to impress Tea Lily, his girlfriend. And I can't believe he's doing this at his age! He must be all of ten, now, isn't he? Time flies so fast. I can't keep up."

"He's eleven, Lotus," her husband, Lionheart, broke in. "I'm proud of that boy, the way he governs his country. He'll make Astrid and Popo a laughingstock, he will."

"Oh, don't say that, Lion!" Lotus Blossom sounded wounded. "He and Popo have been friends since they were tiny kittens. Although I will admit, when Lun puts his mind and heart into something, he does a better than excellent job. Just look at the peace in his country! It's been like that since he became King at age one!"

"That's my boy!" Lionheart exclaimed, grinning. "A chip off the old block!"

"'Old blockhead' is more like it," Shining Moon sniffed.

"Those mountains better be careful, or they'll be hills when he gets through with them," Ah Fu E snorted. He was King Lun's great-grandfather, Shining Moon's father. "That boy doesn't let nothin' stand in his way. If he's determined to jump over the moon, he'll do it. *Why* he wants to do it is subject to speculation, mind you, but I have no doubt that he will succeed."

Other relatives and a couple of friends joined the group. They spoke quietly among themselves so as not to disturb the King's peaceful sleep, and bore Lu Tein's statement true – before going back to sleep themselves, they all placed bets on the degree of their beloved Lun's success. They knew he would do it – by how much was the speculation. It was agreed that Lionheart would accompany him the first day, then Shining Moon, Lotus Blossom, Ah Fu E, and the remaining relatives, each taking a turn per day and night. After all, it wouldn't do to have Lun out of the running if something happened to him before he even got started.

As predicted, the journey to the Butterscotch Mountains was pleasant. They even arrived a day early. Camp appeared at the base of the First Mountain, inside of which lived a spirit dragon. King Lung lit a candle of peace at the edge of the camp to keep it pacified. The dragon read Lun's mind to find out why he was there; like most others, he was amazed at the magnitude of the jump ahead of the King. He decided to assist in the King's training. Dragons are good luck, as everyone knew.

The first day or two was relatively simple. King Lun leaped and played among the rocks of the foothills, getting the feel of them and their energy. The third day, Lu Tein led the King to what looked like a simple, short sheer side of the rock. Told to climb it, King Lun thought, *"Piece of cake."*

An hour later, the side mostly resembled a piece of ragged corduroy, and King Lun's nails were extremely sharp from all the sliding down he did. Frustration and chagrin filled his lithe body.

Lu Tein found a section that was still sheer and scaled it with no problem. King Lun let out a frustrated yowl. His eyes were wide and wild. Lu Tein couldn't keep back a grin as he returned to the King's side.

"How - !" Lun gasped.

Lu Tein extended a pawful of claws.

"Think small," he said. "Come here. I will show you." They went to the place where the gym master climbed. "Look closely here. Yes, this rock is sheer, but here –" he pointed a claw at an almost invisible, extremely tiny pore. "If you think molecular instead of mountain, this becomes simple. When you use the power of your mind to open these infinitesimal orifices, they become big enough to insert a paw, never mind a claw. See them for what they are – the way to scale the side. Meditate on them briefly before beginning the climb. They will show themselves to you, and you can insert your claws easily. Before you try it again, have a few leaps over to those trees a half-mile away to rid your body of the negative energy that now fills it."

King Lun had no trouble following those directions. He came back a little short of breath but willing to tackle what was left of the sheer side. He stared at it, imagined all of the openings just waiting eagerly for his claws, took a deep breath – and climbed. As Lu Tein voiced his original thought, the King smiled a proud-of-himself smile. Lionheart shook his head.

So it went. By the end of the month, after climbing, leaping, swimming, and fighting the spirit dragon, King Lun had conquered the First Mountain. Now it was on to the second.

"Here is where you will put all your training to work toward your goal. See this side of the mountain." He pointed and looked up.

King Lun's eyes followed the point. He looked startled. It looked like a pyramidal stack of layered Lady Fingers, but in reverse. The longest ones were at the top rather than the bottom. He was amazed. Never had he guessed such a fabulous mountain lay within his kingdom. He wanted to do something with or for it, but didn't know what. So he just stared at the Lady Fingers.

"What you will do," Lu Tein said, breaking the King's thoughts into crumbs, "is leap from point to point – which get more pointed as you ascend – to the top. Then you will come back down. I have brought special shoes for you to wear. They will both help and protect you."

King Lun leaped gracefully to the first rounded point, about four feet tall.

"This is not hard, nor is this pointed. So what's the point?"

"These lower rocks are easy. It starts to get hard about a third of the way up. You will not get past there if you do not wear these."

King Lun landed beside his gym master and took one of the shoes into a paw to examine. They were made of hard leather, almost round, with openings for each of his claws to go through. Leather thongs hung from the tops of the shoes, made to be tied around a leg. Behind the openings, tiny metal spikes with broken ends stuck out. The King had never seen anything like this, and looked with wonder at Lu Tein.

"The spikes are to help you grip the tops of the rocks. They are not as round as they look."

"I take it you have done this."

"In order to be a gym master, and yours in particular, yes, I have done this."

The King leaped back up to his previous position. "Where do I go from here?"

"Back down here." It was more of a command than a comment. "You are not to ascend unless you wear these. This mountain has surprises."

"Hey, Kitten," a gentle voice lovingly whispered in Lun's ear. *"Do as he says. The cat knows his stuff. Don't worry, though. I'll be with you if you fall."*

King Lun stopped just before jumping. That voice! Was he hearing things?? His mother had been gone for many years, and this was the first time he'd heard her, although he'd desperately prayed to her when she first joined the ancestors. He was one year old and had just become King. He'd ached for her voice, her guidance. But she'd been silent. To hear her now....

Lun took a deep breath and landed once more beside Lu Tein. The gym master put the shoes on and let the King wobble around the ground a bit to get used to the feel of them.

"They are so difficult to walk in!" the King protested. "How do you do this?"

"Ever walk on concrete in a pair of golf shoes? No? Well, same principle. These are not made for walking. They are made for climbing, so climb already." Lu Tein grinned and pointed upward.

King Lun bowed his head for a moment of prayer. Then he focused his eyes and mind on the "fingers" and began to jump. One by one, he successfully made his way up, zigzagging from one "finger" to another, feeling confident and energetic. He paused, balancing easily on a rounded point, which was not so rounded any more, and surveyed his position. The next "finger" was higher than it looked from the ground, but it was the one he needed to jump to, so he crouched slightly, focused, and leaped. The next moment, he was rapidly descending toward Lu Tein, suddenly slowing as he neared the earth. He flipped his body to land on his feet.

"Ouch!" Lun cried as he hit the ground. The shoes felt like the spikes were being driven into the bottoms of his paws. He rolled quickly to his back, paws waving in the air. Lu Tein came running with a tube of something in his mouth. Quickly he undid all the laces and removed the shoes, tossing them as they came off.

"Hold this," he said to an unseen cat next to him. Lun watched as the cap from the tube stayed in the air where Lu Tein put it. Then a cooling sensation flowed to his mind from each paw in turn. Lu Tein was rubbing something into them.

"What happened?" the King asked, slightly in shock.

"I told you this mountain has surprises. You found one of them." The gym master continued to rub the cream into the paws and up to the ankle joints. "This will ease the muscle strain from when you hit the ground. It's a good thing Lotus Blossom had your back. Literally. She broke your fall so you didn't break your back when you got here."

King Lun looked at the cap, still hovering in the air. He tried to see his mother, but could not.

"Thank you," he whispered.

"You are welcome. Next time, use your meditation before leaping to the next point. The sun's position caused an illusion when it shone on that rock.

There was a ledge there you didn't see. Lu Tein, rub some of that stuff on the top of his head, or he'll have a splitting headache soon."

The cat obeyed. Lun looked like a punk rocker, with his hair standing in spikes on his head and plastered down on his legs so they resembled high boots. He felt himself being lifted from the ground, then carried to his bed in his tent.

"So much for today," a low voice boomed in his ears. *"You need to stay off your feet and let them heal. Don't think too hard, either."* A loud guffaw caused his brain to vibrate. Lun winced. *"Get yourself outside of lots of water and a few extra fish. Sleep. Best thing for you. You'll be good to go tomorrow. Oh, and son–"* the voice paused, then continued quietly, and with pride, *"you do a great job of running the kingdom. We're all very proud of you."* The voice broke on the last word, and then there was silence.

King Lun felt very humbled. He had not expected this at all. Hearing from his parents and knowing that all the ancestors were supporting him gave him a much-needed boost. They were right. He had been overconfident in his abilities and hadn't thought. He was too eager to train. Training the body also meant training the mind. He felt a little foolish for forgetting that, but running a kingdom was not the same thing as running a marathon or running up the side of a mountain. Both needed brains, and sometimes, when training, his remained in the gym bag. He would not make that mistake again. A deep sleep overtook the King. He quickly fell into a party of ancestors making merry at the foot of the Butterscotch Mountains.

Training went easier after that. He thought and meditated briefly before trying the jumps, and Shining Moon and Lotus Blossom caught him when he erred. Skeletons of various animals, including humans, lay in various places the higher he went. They had not been so fortunate to have spirits helping them. King Lun vowed to be more attentive to the ancestors once he returned home.

He discovered that his balance was not what he'd thought it to be. Lu Tein had advised him correctly that the higher the "finger," the pointier the tip. Lun found the shoes very helpful, indeed. They helped him grip the rock points, which were now starting to resemble a sharpened pencil lead. The human philosophical question of how many angels there were on the head of a pin came to mind. He decided it was a foolish question. Even if some angels decided to try to crowd on just for the fun of it – or to make a point – he winced at that thought – it was an inherently foolish thing to do. It had no meaning, as they were impervious to gravity, and since only the winged ones were likely to try, the outcome was moot. Landing on a pointed rock while in training for a spectacular feat had no relation to angels. Had it not been for his ancestral spirits, he would most likely have been one himself now.

Lun's sense of balance became fine-tuned. He experimented with movement on any given point. Some were rounded a bit yet, but now he was close to the top, and the roundness had long since disappeared. Yet the smaller the space, the more confident he felt. All four paws could now fit on a point half the size of a pencil eraser. He knew what the very top would be the hardest. It was the highest leap to the tiniest point. One fraction of an inch in any direction would send him tumbling down. He could not afford to fail.

Lu Tein had not climbed with him, yet King Lun could feel and sometimes hear the gym master giving instructions. Lun was careful to follow them. He did not want to get hurt, and he did not want his mother and grandmother to think less of him. He had no idea how totally amazed they were at his accomplishments and would never think less of him had he fallen to the ground from the very top. Success was not a problem. Lun's physical and mental shape was superb. He would be more than ready to leap over the moon should such an event actually take shape. Shining Moon still thought it was a scam, but she supported her grandson completely in whatever he wanted to do.

King Lun balanced carefully on the penultimate point. One more jump and he'd be at the top. This was indeed hard. He had to leap 55 feet at a five-degree angle and land on literally a pencil point. He thought of an airplane making a perfect three-point landing and wished he'd had a runway instead of a pencil to land on, especially since he had four points instead of three.

"Concentrate on the point and jump. Don't think about your jump; just do it. You have the strength to accomplish that without half trying. See yourself as the angel on the pinpoint. We all know you can do it, but you have to see for yourself that you can." The feeling of Lu Tein's comforting confidence calmed him. *"Think about the end, not getting there. Picture yourself balanced perfectly on the point, and when you feel ready, leap. KEEP THE POINT IN MIND. Do not miss it! You will do it! Leap when you feel ready."*

Lun thought of the sharpened pencil – the VERY sharpened pencil. He pictured himself on top of it, surveying the world he was King of. He saw himself atop the mountain, higher than the mountain. He mentally looked toward his kingdom, lying peacefully in the valley. He could see the larger dot that was his palace and the many dots that made up the town. He saw the lush countryside, the flowing rivers, the forests. A train slowly snaked across the land. His was a beautiful country indeed, and he was proud and happy to live there. He must see it from the very top. King Lun focused his mind and eyes on the mountain before him, preparing the final leap.

All he saw was blue.

"Huh?" he wondered.

Suddenly he realized he was AT the top! He was atop the Second Mountain, balanced on the tiniest point imaginable. Carefully he looked down and got a second surprising realization: the mountain top was flat!

Confusion reigned for a moment. Then reality set in. He was sitting atop a flat space at the very top of the Second Mountain, actually looking at his kingdom! He felt joyous laughter surround him.

"Congratulations! You did it! You conquered the Second Mountain!" Lu Tein's joyous energy surrounded the King. *"I told you this mountain is full of surprises. There's one more. Look behind you."*

King Lun turned. There, between two large rocks several feet away, was the start of a trail that led down the mountainside back to his camp! He felt a lot more laughter, the laughter of joy and success. Everyone was so glad he made it, especially him!

"Can I take these shoes off now?" he questioned.

"Yes, you won't need them on the trail. Come on down!"

Quickly, King Lun removed the shoes. How wonderful the rock felt on his feet. He ran to the trail and began descending. How good it felt to be walking! He broke into a joyful run, stretching and contracting his body to its fullest as he navigated the hiking trail back to the gym master. Surprises, indeed!

A couple of hours later, he was back in camp, tired, happy, and eager both for the next challenge and for bed. Lu Tein gave him a huge hug. He disappeared into his tent and emerged moments later with two bottles of special sparkling ginger water. They downed them without taking a breath.

King Lun collapsed onto the ground. He lay there, feeling the cool earth along his body, smelling the sweetly scented grass, and soaking up the sunshine that edged towards setting. *What a day this is*, he thought. *Certainly, I can jump over the moon! I'm ready NOW. Bring it on!* His thoughts wandered, and he drifted into dreams filled with cows crashing into mountains while he effortlessly scaled them and jumped over them. Astrid looked on, horrified. King Lun smiled a victory smile in his sleep.

The next day was cloudy, and the Third Mountain had disappeared in the fog. The King was certain this was a day for relaxation and recovery, but no, Lu Tein urged him to get up.

"Come, come, we must go. Your third and final challenge awaits. This is the perfect day for it."

The four porters broke camp and followed with the supplies to the base of the Third Mountain. It looked harmless to King Lun, but he had learned that the mountains, so beautiful in the distance, could kill him and feel nothing if he died. They were mounds of unfeeling, uncaring stone that represented in their being the solidity of might combined with size, the challenge to mind and body to overcome obstacles, and the glory of the universe's creation. He wondered what this one had to offer.

The air felt chilly. A light breeze blew the fog around, creating images that changed almost as soon as they formed. This day, the King wore a long-sleeved nylon top with a form-fitting long-legged nylon bottom. It kept him warm, although his paws felt cool.

Everyone ate silently. Lun sensed the ancestors were present, but they, too, felt a bit down. There was little conversation among them.

After the meal, Lu Tein consulted a chart of the mountains. He looked up, but could not see anything. He turned back to the chart and studied it. After a while, he said, "Come."

King Lun followed him a short distance to a couple of similar-sized rocks that gave him the impression of sentinels guarding a gate.

"That's right." Lu Tein said. "These are known as the Twin Guardians. They protect this trail up the mountain from those who would harm it. It is a mystery how they do it, but they seem to be able to sense the energy of the person who would climb and emit their own combining energy to prevent the passage of those who are planning mischief either to the mountain or to peaceful climbers. They will let you pass with no problem. This trail goes straight up to the top. It winds up, down, around; you will see some most astoundingly beautiful sights on your way up. The way back is the same. All you need to do is walk up without stopping and turn around and come back. It should take you about five hours to the top, given a steady walking pace. I hope to see you back here about two hours after the sun sets."

"What do I take with me?"

"Two bottles of water, one for up, one for down. Be sure to ration the water carefully. If it is gone before you reach the bottom, I cannot bring you more. The Guardians will not let me pass."

King Lun looked at him, incredulous.

"But you are my instructor and friend. You would not hurt a fly. Why can you not pass?"

"Because I am not on trial here, you are. The hikers are merely hikers, but the sentinels and the mountain know that you have come to learn, to test yourself, to become the best you that you can be. Even the Ancestors do not dare help you. This time, you are on your own. You are smart and confident, King Lun. The mountain should not be a problem for you."

"Then what is my challenge?"

"Yourself."

Lu Tein placed his paws on the King's shoulders.

"Remember, my friend, the mountain is here only to test you. I do not know what challenges you will face, but whatever they are, fear not and face them bravely. You are the most beautiful model of a true, wholly connected cat, not just to yourself and your subjects, but also to your ancestors. As King, you embody not just the earthly realm, but the universe and its glories as well. The mountain is one of the glories. If you connect with it, nothing can stop you from achieving whatever you put your mind to. Given the nature of the world, there is much good you can do to defeat the evil that is encroaching on it. Your world is about to change, my friend. Go. Remember – walk up, walk down. Period. And ration the water. It is of the utmost importance that you do so. One bottle up, one bottle down." He gave the King a big bear hug.

King Lun felt awed. Surely Lu Tein exaggerated. A mountain as beautiful as this one could not possibly have tests that were difficult. What could he encounter except a few hikers? As for the water, he had tested himself periodically, going for two to three days without drinking, yet keeping a normal kingly schedule. Surely ten hours would not be a challenge. Or…?

"Do not worry, Lu Tein," Lun said confidently. "I shall see you soon." With a big grin on his face, a bottle of water in each paw, he gave a wave as he passed between the sentinels for his final test.

It seemed to him as he passed the stones and started up the trail that he had gone inside the mountain, but how could that be? The sun was now high in the sky, the fog had disappeared, and the trail lay straight before him. A five hour walk was not a problem. The trail wasn't even steep. Piece of cake.

Wait. The King had a mental pause. It seemed like he'd said that before, and the cake wasn't as light and fluffy as it should have been. In fact, it was hard as a – well, rock. But here, amid the flowers and grass, even a small brook that flowed alongside the trail, everything seemed peaceful and calm. Why was he feeling doubtful? *No negative thoughts allowed,* he told himself, continuing on.

He thought of his kingdom. As loved as he was by his subjects, so he loved them in return. To see them happy was his greatest joy, and he provided well for them. Oops. King Lun remembered with embarrassment his total absorption in training when he neglected to notice that things were not going well. He also remembered his attitude, snapping at the advisors and other employees, and that awful encounter with the koi pond he'd just as soon forget. Determined not to let that happen again, Lun would become very careful how he responded to his subjects in the future. Once this is over, he thought, he would go back to his peaceful, loving self, caring for one and all and swinging and singing each night to his beloved moon. He was here now on his last journey to reaching his goal of jumping over his friend, and if all he had to do was to walk to the top and back, that surely could be done easily, given all he'd accomplished before.

He was warm in his nylon outfit, so he stopped and had a sip of water. A couple of hikers passed him going down, and they exchanged pleasantries. The King smiled and hummed as he walked, taking in the majesty of the surrounding peaks, a few topped with snow. The trail became broader as it entered the foothills, and the scenery changed. Grass gave way to gravel, and the brook disappeared into an underground waterway, falling gently into a hole in the side of the upcoming rock. He followed the trail around the rock and encountered his first obstacle.

A kitten.

His heart melted.

The tiny animal apparently had gotten a paw stuck in a crack in a rock. Knowing well how kittens were curious and had to try out everything, he wasn't surprised at this. What should have surprised him and warned him was that the kitten was there in the first place. What idea came to him was why the hikers, whom he recently passed, didn't stop to help. A tiny mew refocused his attention to its plight. He was about to stop and extricate it when a large crow flew close, cawing loudly, distracting the King. He ducked sideways and moved forward to get out of its way. When he looked back at the kitten, it was gone. Then he remembered Lu Tein's words: "keep walking." So he did.

Pondering on this, King Lun almost stumbled over a tree branch that had fallen onto the path from a tree growing out of the gravel and rocks above left. He looked at it while maneuvering around the branch, wondering if it would disappear in front of his eyes, but it didn't. It was a real tree.

The King shook his head and concentrated on his goal: keep walking to the top, turn around, and come down. Still moving, he closed his eyes briefly and said a prayer. He opened them in time to keep from walking straight over a ledge that the trail now led up to, and around, a wall of rock.

"Jeepers!" he said aloud. "Focus, Lun, focus!" He knew he could, so he placed his goal in front of his eyes and walked steadily toward it.

The trail wound around the sheer rock to his left. To his right was a drop-off, and he didn't want to know how far down it went. Farther off were First and Second Mountains, and he remembered his trials and conquering them. He would conquer this, too. The King continued focusing on walking to the top.

Steadily the trail climbed. It wasn't a steep climb, but he could feel the tension in his legs. He shook each in turn as he stepped forward. The trail narrowed, and he slowed his pace. Would it come to an end, or would it widen again to reveal another beautiful side of this mountain? He hoped for the latter and mentally prepared for the former, which turned out to be a wise move.

The trail ended abruptly after the next bend. What in--?? King Lun looked around, at the sheer wall next to him, its height, and then he looked down. Big mistake. Below him was a thick mist that obscured everything. He had to go up or back. Back was not an option, especially when he turned to see what was behind him.

Nothing.

He was standing on a piece of rock big enough to hold him. That was it. How could this be!? A few minutes ago, he was admiring the beautiful scenery and now.... *Focus, Lun.* He went inside of himself to find peace. He concentrated on it and found courage and bravery. Holding to all of these, he opened his eyes, stuck one water bottle in his mouth and the other in his belt, and leaped up. He grabbed the side of the mountain in his claws and climbed. He didn't realize the façade gradually curved over the little ledge until he saw the mist above him when it should have been below. Reinforcing his determination, Lun kept going until he ran out of rock.

Oh, jeez. Oh, yes! Safety in the form of another wide trail lay a few feet to his right. The jump was an easy distance – wait. All four paws clung to rock, and he had no idea how far down was. With the added encumbrance of two water bottles, neither of which he planned to lose, what should have been an easy five-foot leap was now a lesson in logistics. Again, Lun went inside of himself. He saw where he was, where he wanted to go, and, blessings to God, the way to get there. Unhooking one paw from the rock, he placed the water bottle in his mouth under his belt on his left side, crawled sideways one foot, and, using his hind legs as a springboard, leaped from the rock to the trail, landing easily on all fours. Moving that extra foot to the right gave him the perspective he needed to see everything around him clearly, and the trail was actually only about three feet away and a foot down. Sunlight could create some interesting illusions, he decided.

After another sip of water, he again walked confidently along. The rock to his right was jagged, but the wide ledge gave him room to avoid sharp edges. Tips of trees appeared to his left and grew until he again was on flat land. With an open expanse to his right, Lun realized he was on a plateau. Again, sunlight streamed down, warming him. Two more sips of water were required. He checked the level. Still three-quarters full. Good. He looked around and saw grass, forest, and high mountains surrounding him. The top of a distant one sparkled with snow. Farther to his right, another top was lost to fog. To his left, the Third Mountain rose with a rare beauty, as veins of precious stones snaked across its peak, colors caught by sunbeams. He paused momentarily to admire it. The world contained marvels of nature not seen in his kingdom. Lun took one more sip and continued his journey.

The walk through the forest was without incident. On the other side, a long, large lake suddenly appeared. Although the sun could not be seen, the water seemed to sparkle. Small boats dotted the surface here and there, containing humans who fished. They were far away from the shore. Farther down, a pickup truck sat near the water, two humans grilling their catch. The scent caught Lun's nose, and he became aware of a craving hunger. It drew him nearer to the pickup than was prudent for a cat on a journey, but even though he kept his mind on his goal, his stomach seemed to have other plans. The hair on the back of his neck prickled, and he veered away just in time. A fishing hook with sinker landed inches from his face, so he ran back to the trail and continued running for a distance. Forest again protected him, and as long as he kept to the weaving trail, he was safe.

Phew! Lun thought. Pausing long enough for another sip, he walked on. *Stay safe, Lun. You don't want to make a fatal mistake now. Focus!*

The forest thinned to where he was once again on rock. Darkness approached. A strange feeling seeped into him. His excellent night vision momentarily intensified, giving him an exact picture of where he walked: trail straight ahead through rocks and scrub, disappearing around another curve as it rose to meet the mountain. Then everything blurred.

Nerves and whiskers on alert, King Lun proceeded slowly. His ears on alert for any sound, body sensitive for any vibration, he felt himself begin to climb.

The trail grew rougher underfoot as it went higher. It seemed to blend into the mountain, reminding Lun of his attempts to scale the Second Mountain. This was easier. There were many small 'fingers' to grasp. He sensed height, though how high was uncertain. Still he climbed. Then something brushed his side. He stretched a paw to feel it. It felt the same as whatever he clung to, and he stretched out a front leg to see where it went. It seemed parallel to whatever he climbed, which by now, between the descended darkness and his blurred vision, he could not see. Slower now, Lun continued careful progress. The thing at his side began to press in, and soon he could not move. Wherever he was was too narrow to pass. He tried moving right. Nope. Then he tried moving left. That seemed more open, but a water bottle caught on one of the "fingers" and he had a little trouble releasing it. He moved back to where he'd been, and that did it.

But that meant he was stuck.

Somehow, the trail had led him to a dead end. This did not seem logical. Carefully, bracing against the object now behind him, King Lun extended both front legs and paws to feel where he was. It appeared he was captured between two trails; the air told him he'd ascended quite a bit higher, but into what? A cave, perhaps? This seemed possible, but cave walls would be a lot smoother than what he felt. A cold breeze came up. This did not have the characteristics of a cave breeze. It was an open breeze, confirmed when his captive position swayed a bit, still keeping him prisoner. Even though he couldn't really see anything, King Lun looked around and up. Wait. There seemed to be a light above him. He tried to move toward it and found he couldn't. He tried moving back down. That didn't work either.

He was definitely stuck.

So he went inside himself and concentrated on moving one of the obstacles. He decided to move the one on his back, as that had gradually pressed harder, causing the predicament. He pictured it moving backward, away from his now aggravated spine and felt the pressure lessen. Being in control of the object, he moved it far enough away from him to allow him free movement. But the object came back and hit him in the side, almost knocking him away from whatever he clung to. Startled, Lun dug his claws in. Something about it felt familiar. His muscles began to complain, but he didn't dare let go. Carefully he moved left.

Then he ran out of object.

Now he was upside down, clinging by his hind paws. He felt something slip from his belt and tried to grab it. It felt slippery, and he fumbled it. It slid from his grasp and fell – where? There was momentarily no sound, then a rustle below him, and a sequence of rustles growing quieter one by one until there was only silence.

He realized he was not on a trail. He had climbed something. He sniffed. Yes!

The thin air, the warm scent of pine – he had climbed a tree!

Suddenly his vision cleared. How in the world had he gotten up here? The light above was his beloved moon, watching over him. Lun climbed higher until he could clearly see everything from an open branch. He was very near the top of an old tree that had grown out of the side of the mountain, as they sometimes do. Other trees from the plateau below grew up alongside it, forming an aerial forest. Of all things. King Lun had to laugh with relief and humor. He must have somehow gotten onto a large root and followed it up here. Another tree swayed very close to his perch, and he saw that's how he'd gotten stuck. The space between the two was quite narrow. He looked toward the mountain. A few feet above him was the trail he should have been on before taking this unusual short cut. Lun balanced and leaped onto it. Then he discovered he'd lost his full water bottle.

Annoyed, he took a sip from the remaining one. Half full. But he wasn't far from the top now, so he didn't worry. The moonlight was bright and lit the way for him. He sang a favorite song to it, thanking it for the light. The moon seemed to glow a bit more, then return to normal. It pleased King Lun.

A short time later, the trail ended at the top. Lun looked around for a few moments, then started back down. He had no idea how long it took him to get up there, but Lu Tein had said five hours, so that must be right. Mentally prepared for the trees again, he did not expect to find a regular trail that kept him steadily descending, encountering no problems.

Until he came across desert halfway down.

Deserts during the day are hot, but at night they can be bone-chilling cold. The King was still a couple thousand feet up, and this desert was no exception. The nylon workout suit he wore – where it wasn't torn or holey – kept him warm for a short time, but soon he began to feel chilly. Then cold. Then freezing. Body shivering and teeth chattering hard, Lun wanted only to lie down somewhere in some shelter and sleep. But there was no shelter, only interminable miles of sand, cacti, scrub, and rocks. Small stones and larger rocks that caused him to slip tore at the pads of his feet. Lun looked at the sky. His moon gave him light to see by, but that was all; even it seemed cold and distant. He stopped for a sip of water. Warm or of moderate temperature earlier, it felt now like ice. He saw himself as a snowman, or snowcat, and certainly felt like it. Lun's pace was now more of a crawl as he tried to fluff out his fur to stave off the cold. Finally, his frozen mind realized it could engulf him in a mental fire, which he then created. A few minutes later, he was walking close to his former pace, seeing himself surrounded by flames that produced a glowing warmth throughout his body. He took another sip of water and checked the level. Just under half. He should have enough to get back to camp.

But where was camp? There was no trail. He'd just walked into the desert and not paid attention to see when he got off track. His mind searched for a possible answer, but there wasn't any. He looked around. The moon was partially behind one of the mountains now, and the added darkness didn't really help, even if he did have great night vision. The mountains were black zigzags against a star-filled night. The King checked for a familiar constellation, figuring he could get his bearings by it. He saw some, but there were many he did not know, being in a very different part of his country now. He wasn't sure which direction was which. The moon rose in the west and set in the east at this time of year, but being surrounded by mountains made it difficult to tell any direction.

The moon seemed to peer at him before disappearing completely from view. All he had left was starlight, which wasn't much help. He searched for a certain constellation which, at this time of year, should have been about a forty-five-degree angle from the earth, but was at a sixty-degree angle instead. Indeed, all the stars seemed to be in different places; even a shooting star appeared to be going in the wrong direction. Not only that, but the mountain the moon had slipped behind began to glow with a rising sun. If that truly were east, that meant that King Lun had spent the last hour, at least, going the wrong way. He should have been heading south.

Turning a quarter turn, the King began hiking in a southerly direction. That didn't feel right, either. *Think, Lun, stop and think.* He sat, waiting for the sun to rise.

It didn't.

One by one, the stars twinkled out until the sky was totally black. Oh, great. He was sitting in the middle of a desert, surrounded by mountains, no moon, no stars, no sun, and no sense of where he was. Mind and body went on full alert. No sound escaped him, no scent was too faint for his nose. He heard the scuttling of insects and small creatures around him, noted a flower on a blooming cactus off to his right. Other than that, the silence was deafening.

The pupils in King Lun's cat eyes opened wide. He could now see the outline of the mountains against the sky. Slowly he turned to try to get his bearings. If he could remember the shape of the mountains as he came into the desert, he would know which way to walk. He'd seen their outline on his way down the trail, but the trail had turned – yes! Find the outline and then turn his body in the direction of the trail! He set his mind and eyes to work together. Slowly he turned, watching, looking, searching – there! This is what they looked like a few minutes before entering the desert. Count the seconds…turn right! Again the outline presented itself. Count…turn left and right again… Yes! Keeping his mind focused on the silhouette, he counted – got it! The King knew which way to go. The stars reappeared in clusters, and the moon rose above one of the mountains, giving a bit of light to the desert floor. Lun started off confidently again. He no longer needed the trail to find his way back. But he could use another sip of water….

He took a gulp and held the bottle up. He could not see the level. It was not quite light enough. So he felt the bottle with a paw. The water was colder than the rest of its container. About one-third full. King Lun was not sure how much farther he had to travel, but this amount should be enough to get him back to Lu Tein. He had done well with the water conservation, and that pleased him, considering he'd dropped a full bottle several hours previously. His slightly dry throat asked for one more gulp, but the King ignored the feeling. There would be plenty to drink once he stepped clear of the Guardian rocks.

The sun began to rise to his left. King Lun once more checked the silhouette of the mountains and turned slightly left. If he returned to Lu Tein according to the instructor's comments, he should be back on – wait! Lu Tein said he should be back two hours after the sun set, not rose. That meant he was half a day behind! What in the world had happened to the time??

The King began to run. His instructor would be very worried about him, since he did not show up when expected. The realization that he was truly alone against the elements flooded his body, not just his mind. Lun had faced challenges before, but this was the first time there was absolutely no help available. He felt very alone, but not frightened. At least, not yet.

The desert began to warm under the sun's rays. Lun resumed walking. Since he was already late, there was no sense in wearing himself out. He was able to judge the distance yet to travel – about another hour or possibly two, max. He wondered if he'd have enough water to get back, then scolded himself. He reminded himself he'd gone for three days with no liquid, but that was different. It was a personal test, water was readily available, and he could decide to quit at any time. Here, there was no quitting.

Lun's pace slowed. The desert was definitely warmer now. His fur would keep him from getting sunburned, but the nylon top began creating problems for his body. He took a small sip of water. The distance did not seem to have lessened. When would he get to the trees and bridges and ponds again? The heat intensified. The King stopped and removed the nylon top. Coolness felt good. He continued on.

It seemed like no time had passed before he took off the bottoms. His sense of right did not want to leave the clothing litter the desert, but there was no reason for him to actually carry them back. They were torn, anyway. He took another sip. One-quarter full. This should be enough. Shouldn't it? Had to be enough!

A shadow passed over. King Lun looked up. A very large black bird seemed interested in him. It circled slowly, then flew away. Lun checked the silhouette again. Turn right. He changed his direction slightly. A little more. Back on track.

Although the sun hadn't moved from its previous position – or it seemed that way, probably because of the change of direction – the temperature kept rising. Since his kingdom never got really very hot or very cold, King Lun had no reference to go by regarding how to handle it. He saw a bit of shade from a saguaro and sat in it to think through his situation. Logically, it wasn't good. Physically, it wasn't good. Same for emotionally. Spiritually, he wasn't quite sure yet, but he had a hunch that wasn't good, either. He mentally went inside of himself for a brief meditation. His brain said, *find shelter and wait until darkness when it's cooler.* His body said, *I can make it for a while yet. Stay and rest awhile, then go on.* His emotions said, *I am in a very dangerous predicament. There is a chance I will not make it back.* His spirit said, *Trust me. I am your Self. We will make it if you listen to me. I will not fail you.* The King came back to the desert reality and rested for a bit, staying in the cactus' shadow. When he felt that it was time to go on, he got up, found his bearings, and started walking.

It got hotter. Soon the water was gone. He seemed to be no closer to the exit than before. Lun thought of his moon and began to sing. A lizard raised its head from the rock on which it lay and listened. The head moved to the rhythm of the song. King Lun acknowledged the lizard with a wave of a paw. When he stopped a moment later, the lizard flicked itself off the rock and disappeared under the sand.

Again, the King sang. But singing made him thirsty. Oh, good! There was a pool of water up ahead! He started for it, then stopped. It is an illusion, his spirit said. He continued on, checking the silhouette of the mountains periodically. Something was not right. He was certain he was moving correctly across the desert, yet did not seem to be going anywhere.

An Ancestor appeared before him. Although there was no speech, it seemed to mouth 'Go this way' and waved a spectral arm in the direction Lun should take. The mountains did seem much closer there, and for a moment, the King thought of going in the indicated direction. His mind said, "The Ancestors cannot help you." That was correct. King Lun replied, "I cannot. Begone, evil spirit. You cannot trick me." The Ancestor vanished.

My mind is playing tricks on me, Lun thought. *Focus. Focus on your reason for doing this. I am strong. I will find the right path out of here, and all will be well. I shall jump over the moon ten times higher than the cow. A cow! No piece of dog meat is going to beat me!*

A half-hour later, he'd changed his mind.

The heat was oppressive. No breeze, no water. Waves of heat rose in front of him. His body felt like a rag. Lun thought of Astrid and saw her in front of him, chewing his flowers and smiling a contented smile. He attempted to hit her, but she was no longer there. Instead, he lost his balance and fell into the sand.

A saguaro beckoned him. He crawled to it. It unzipped itself and opened its body. Cool water splashed over the King. He stuck his head inside the cactus and drank his fill. Thanking the spirits of Life, the King lay in the cactus's shadow. He was momentarily at peace. Then heavy thirst hit him, and he realized he had not drunk at all. He spit as much sand as he could from this mouth. The fountain had been another illusion. His brain said, *Not so much. Use your claws. This cactus does contain water.*

The King clawed the cactus, being careful of its thick spines. There was water inside, and he squeezed it into his sandy mouth. But he could not drink sand, so he spit it out again. He did this twice more before the cactus dried up. No more water.

The sun was in setting mode, so King Lun, after once again checking his position, kept on toward the Guardians. Other illusions beckoned him to a soft bed, a bath, a banquet table – he suddenly felt ravenously hungry – and shade. He banished them all and forced himself forward. A rock appeared in front of his face. He swung a paw at it, and it vanished. Desert animal sounds increased in intensity until they became a cacophony of insanity. The King tried to scream but could not. He kept crawling forward. Another rock appeared. He swiped at it and twisted in pain. This one was real!

A path lay in front of him. He crawled along, mouth and throat parched, body hot and sore, and ignored by hikers and others who now shared the path. Several times they just missed stepping on him. *There is no help,* a voice chanted over and over. *They do not see you. You are nonexistent. Give up this ridiculous quest. There is no way out. See for yourself.*

The King raised his head and looked through dry, gritty eyes at his surroundings. The voice seemed to be telling the truth. No one saw him. A man stepped on his tail. Lun tried to scream, but no sound came. Humans and animals seemed to come and go at will, passing through the rock for entry and exit.

Impossible, his mind said.

Correct, his spirit replied. *Remember who you are, King Lun. Know that I am with you and will bring you out of this. Remember your quest. Trust in it. Trust in me. You will emerge victorious.*

Shapes swam before King Lun's eyes. The rocks of the mountain wavered in the heat. King Lun thought of his beloved moon, his garden, his people, his palace. He thought of King Popo and Astrid. He barely had the energy to see inside of himself, but he did see and saw a strong young King sitting on a gold and marble throne, with his subjects gathered around chanting, "We love you." He knew this to be true, so he kept pushing himself forward. Thirst raked his throat; breathing began to hurt. His lungs hurt; everything hurt.

Then he saw them: the Guardians. They seemed an impossible distance in front of him, but they were there, and it gave him hope. Pushing himself with whatever strength he had left, Lun inched toward the opening. It was dark beyond, but Lu Tein was there: Lun felt rather than saw the master. Total exhaustion consumed him. If only he could rest for just a moment, just close his eyes for one second, but something inside would not let him. He felt so dried up. His mouth was cracked. He could not cry out to his friend. He pushed himself another few inches, feeling the pain of being stepped on constantly by uncaring, unseeing humans, but he was back now. Just a few more feet…crawling, pushing, a half-inch at a time, a half-inch, just a couple more feet…the Guardians were there… keep going…death made its presence known, and he saw the Ancestors anxiously waiting, arms outstretched… oh, the peace of joining them… they wavered, undulated in front of dry, sand-filled eyes…a few more inches…the goal floated in front of him…inch…inch…Lun stretched out a paw…I hurt…my body screams with pain…inch…he stretched and extended a claw to touch the ground in front of the Guardians…he felt his body being lifted and gave himself up to the light that waited to greet him.

Eventually, a conglomeration of soft voices penetrated his unconsciousness, gradually sorting themselves out into voices he recognized. Lu Tein's was the loudest, and King Lun felt momentarily horrified that his good friend had joined him in death. The voices became clear, and he heard sentences bemoaning his fate and also congratulating him on achieving victory.

King Lun gradually became conscious of himself. He lay on something very soft. It was a cloud, for Heaven is where he believed himself to be.

Tentatively moving first paws and then his body, he slowly became fully aware of his surroundings.

It seemed he had not died after all.

"He is awake," Lotus Blossom said softly.

Lun opened a crusty eye and attempted to focus on the colorful shape which swayed before him.

"Mother?"

"I'm here, my son." Her voice was a delicate whisper. "We are all so proud of you. You have achieved greatness, not only in this world but also the next."

King Lun opened the other crusty eye. Still swaying slightly, Lotus Blossom's figure cleared up.

"Which world am I in? Is my kingdom still intact? Are my subjects well?"

Shining Moon stuck her face right in front of his.

"Your kingdom is fine, and so are your subjects. You'll be fine in a few days. Congrats, my boy. You did spectacularly."

King Lun took a deep breath. Breathing did not hurt. He raised his head and saw a beaming Lu Tein and all the ancestors gathered around him, huge smiles on their faces.

"Lie down, me bucko," Flying Tiger boomed. "Give yourself a couple of days, and you'll be right as rain. You came down off that mountain in record time. There were a couple of obstacles, of course, but you dealt with them as if they were merely gnats flying in your face. Well done!"

The King yawned. "Excuse me, but what is well done?"

"Your challenge," Lu Tein exclaimed. "You went to the top of the Third Mountain and came back while it was still daylight! Magnificent!"

The King yawned again. He felt groggy and a little lightheaded. "Can we discuss this another time?" he asked. "I beg your humble forgiveness, but I do not feel very well."

"Understandable," Lu Tein agreed. "Very well, everyone. Come back in a couple of days after our King has had a chance to recuperate. Then we'll fill him in."

Murmuring congratulations, the Ancestors faded away. King Lun fell back to sleep immediately.

A full day went by before he awoke.

"Lu Tein!" he croaked. "I need water!"

The gym master immediately set a bowl before him. The King drank it dry. Then he drank a second. He fell asleep again.

The morning sun hung low in the sky when the King opened his eyes. He stretched and yawned. Lu Tein was preparing breakfast a few feet away. He glanced at Lun's stretching figure.

"Good morning. How do you feel?"

"Good. No, wonderful!" He yawned again. "Did I sleep through the night?"

"A whole day and a night," the gym master said. "Here is your breakfast: scrambled egg with a protein powder milkshake. Won't do to eat too much today. Tomorrow, start eating again like you usually do." He brought Lun a scrambled egg on a plate and the shake in a fountain container with straw.

"You need to take a short walk after breakfast. Do them periodically throughout the day to get your muscles up and limber again. I've been rubbing you with a special cream to help your muscles stay limber. Eat, and then we'll talk."

Lun nodded and devoured the breakfast in no time. He stretched again and rose.

"How does standing feel?"

Lun turned into himself. "Good. I think I can walk today. How far?"

"Just around camp at first. By tomorrow you should be able to hike the trail to the lake and back. After that, we'll get you really up and running."

The Ancestors floated in. After much congratulatory greeting, they accompanied Lun in his first jaunt around the camp area. Then they sat him down and told him all about what happened. Lun was stunned when they finished.

"I did all that!?"

Flying Tiger slapped him on the back. "You certainly did, my boy! We're all prouder than a flock of peacocks over your accomplishments!

Why, you'll have that silly cow so mortified when she sees you jump, she'll go away and join a herd of – of - " He scratched his head, looking puzzled.

"Sheep, if she can find a flock big enough to equal the sheepishness she'll feel after you soar a mile over that moon!" Lotus Blossom stated firmly.

"Oh, my." Lun looked bemused. "Am I really going to do that?"

"Of course you are!" Flying Tiger thundered. "What do you think you've done all this training for!?"

"Training?"

There was a sudden silence. The Ancestors looked at each other as if someone else had asked the question.

"Lun, darling," Lotus Blossom began, "do you know who we are?"

"Why, yes, you're my mother, you're my father, and I think you are that nice lady who likes to plant trees in the palace garden." Lun pointed at his grandmother. "I seem to remember you doing that a long time ago. Is that still your occupation?"

Shining Moon looked at him, disgusted. "I gave that up a long time ago, Lun. If I didn't know better, I'd say you have gone bananas!"

"Mother!" Lotus Blossom scolded. She turned back to King Lun.

"Walk with us, dear. Let's talk about things."

"Sure." King Lun got up. "Where are we going?"

"Oh, just around. We'd like to fill you in on a few things."

"Then let's get started. Lead the way."

They walked around the camp, back up the hiking trail to the lake inside of the Third Mountain, back to camp, and then down the road for a while, Lotus Blossom and King Lun beside her leading the way, the Ancestors crowding around and floating along behind. By the time the walk was done, Lun had recalled everything and was his old, eager self.

"Tomorrow we leave for King Popo's palace," Lu Tein said. "You must start your final week of preparation."

King Lun was ready.

They broke camp the following day and took their time getting to the palace, arriving two days before King Lun was to challenge Astrid.

The two Kings were happy to see each other again and spent some time reminiscing before Lu Tein reminded King Lun why he was there.

"Oh, yes. Popo, my friend, I am here to challenge Astrid's jump."

"You!?" King Popo was astonished. Then he began to laugh.

"Lun, old chap, I do believe you're off your chump! Why, you're so tiny compared to her, you'd do well to jump over my baby bamboo bush in the hallway. It takes muscle, old friend, to do something like that!"

"Still, there are two days left to the challenge, and I declare that I challenge Astrid's jump!" King Lun announced loudly.

Two more days, and I'll have me a new servant and a fantastic cow, King Popo thought.

"I accept your challenge," he told King Lun.

"I will spend tomorrow in meditation, and tomorrow night I will jump," Lun stated.

"Of course! But tonight, in honor of your visit, we shall feast!"

"I am sorry, my friend, but I must eat properly tonight and tomorrow. I will sit in on your feast, but I will eat only what my gym instructor, Lu Tein, prepares for me. I must be in my best form."

King Popo was taken aback, but agreed.

The following evening was calm and cool, with a slight breeze. King Lun inquired about Astrid's highest jump.

"Still pretty much on track, old boy," Popo replied. "Doing a hundred feet or so."

"Then I don't have to exert myself too much," Lun smiled.

Popo laughed and gave him a slap on the back.

"Good one, Lun!" he chuckled. "So when do you propose to jump?"

"I will consult How Fat and Lu Tein. They will advise me of the best time."

"Go for it."

Popo was not concerned. He and King Lun had been kittens together. Popo had been the active one, while Lun preferred quiet activities involving books. After Lun's father passed away, and he became King, Popo and his family took leave and moved to their present location. Popo became King a year after a relative died and left the kingdom to him.

They'd lost touch after a couple of years. Lun had begun training with the gym master, enough to keep in good physical shape. He still preferred quiet activities and books. But he was not about to let this challenge go by. A point of honor was at stake: his own beliefs in his independence and prowess.

Three hours later, the moon was high. Everyone came out to see King Lun jump. He was sitting in the back garden sphinxlike, turned into himself, wearing a white reflective, flame-resistant, tightly fitting top and pants. When the commotion of the crowd interfered, he came back to his regular self and stood.

"Ladies and Gentlemen!" Popo roared. The crowd grew silent. "As you know, tomorrow will be the one year anniversary of my challenge. My good friend, King Lun of the neighboring kingdom, has offered tonight to equal or beat Astrid's feat of jumping over the moon."

Cheers, clapping, and good wishes interrupted the speech.

"Be that as it may –" he raised his paws for silence – "I never expected a challenger, especially my good friend, here. So here is the deal: King Lun will attempt momentarily to jump over the moon. If he succeeds and beats Astrid's jumps, he will get this fine farmer here as his servant and Astrid. If he fails, I get a new servant and Astrid. We want to keep this fine cow in our kingdom, do we not?"

A roar of assent arose.

"But a deal is a deal," Popo continued. "If King Lun beats Astrid's jump, he will be declared the winner, and it's winner take all!"

King Lun chuckled inwardly. He didn't need the money Astrid's feat brought into the kingdom, and he didn't need a cow that ate prized flowers. He had his own ideas about winning.

"I am ready."

"Give the King some room here!" King Popo cried. Everyone backed off to give Lun the space he needed.

Lun went into himself. He saw himself clear the moon by a mile and smiled. After directing power to his hind legs and mentally preparing his body, Lun came back out, turned, and faced the moon…

...and leaped atop the nearest tree, bounded over the treetops, and used the back wall as a launch. He did this so fast that some of the onlookers thought he made himself invisible.

"There he is!" cried someone in the crowd, pointing to a rapidly disappearing white speck in the sky.

They all watched keenly and silently as King Lun shot toward the moon. Soon his shadow appeared on the moon's surface, but a white speck appeared some distance above. The arc of his jump could be clearly seen because of the reflective suit. A few moments later, he started his descent. There was a momentary burst of orange as he reentered the earth's atmosphere, and then the white speck reappeared, gradually growing larger. It disappeared behind the faraway treetops some minutes later.

Astrid couldn't believe her eyes. How could this piece of mouse bait beat her?? This was impossible! She was big and powerful!! She was mortified. Beaten by a small cat!!!

The farmer knew he would be spending the rest of his life serving this King Lun. But he'd gotten to know King Popo well during the year, and was relieved he didn't have to be a servant to HIM!

King Popo just stood there gawking, mouth open, eyes wide. His mind could not adjust to this event. He was so sure he'd get a servant... and a cash cow.

He needn't have worried. King Lun refused the prize. Popo got to keep Astrid, who would keep bringing money into the kingdom through her special talent, the farmer got a paying position as head gardener, and King Lun went back to his peaceful kingdom, bringing honor to his species by his magnificent jump and to his ancestors by being himself.

Life went on as usual in both kingdoms.

Until...

A few months after the event, Flying Tiger cornered his son in the bath and asked, "When are you going to take a wife? Won't live forever, you know! Need an heir to rule the kingdom!"

Lun was stunned.

"A wife!" he gasped, recalling some of the horror stories shared by his male Ancestors and living constituents.

Flying Tiger was not able to escape the tidal wave created as a pale wet blur leaped through the window and over several trees, disappearing beyond the horizon.

He shook off the water and stared after his son.

"What'd I say?" he wondered. "All I mentioned was for him to start thinking about a wife, or at least a female friend...."

But that's another story.

About the Author

Bella Karoli was reared in the Midwest, an only child. Her father wanted a boy, so among the dolls and stuffed animals was a large metal red fire engine with a siren and a ladder that turned all directions and extended, and an Erector set. He also taught her how to shoot and bought her own BB gun, air rifle, and a cap gun. She knew how to use standard household tools by the age of four, so she took the wheels off her coaster wagon and put them on a large box, pulling it through the house with a piece of clothesline.

She also liked to build models of planes and cars.

In third grade, she started writing poems. She also had been taking accordion lessons for about a year, so she set a poem in one of her mother's magazines to music. That started her on composing. At thirteen, a picture of her sitting on her 1919 Allis Chalmers Model B tractor and a poem she had written about steam engines appeared in a trade magazine. At the time, she was a charter member of an early gas and steam engine club.

Bella preferred individual sports like badminton and bowling while growing up. Not really knowing what she wanted to do with her life, she entered college with the idea of becoming a college professor, but had to switch to a German major from English because she couldn't write term papers. Her primary writing was and is creative, and while getting a Master's degree recently, in one of her first classes, she accidentally turned the end of the final paper into a story!

In her late 30's, Bella went back to school to get a Music Therapy degree, but a move to California and being hired by its largest HMO full time ended that idea. After 17 years, she and her mother moved to Arizona. Mom passed away four years later, and she moved to Las Vegas. That is where she started working on the Master's degree while working for the school district as a substitute special ed teacher's aide. At the advice of a friend, she moved back to Arizona where living was cheaper. Two years later, she had the degree and moved back to the greater Las Vegas area. She currently lives with her partner and best friend, who encourages and supports her in many ways as she works to find her new niche in the creative writing world.